The Hail You Say

Book 5 of The Hail Raisers

By

Lani Lynn Vale

ISBN-13:
978-1981981960

ISBN-10:
1981981969

Dedication

To my son.

My favorite superhero is Thor—Yes, because he has a beard.

My least favorite superhero is Iron Man—mainly because he's short.

No, that hasn't changed today. Yes, you can stop asking me. No, I won't mind if you ask me again tomorrow because I love you.

Acknowledgements

Stu Reardon - Model

Golden Czermak - Photographer

Danielle Palmumbo - My awesome content editor

Ink it out Editing & Kellie Montgomery—Editors

My mom - Thank you for reading this book eight million two hundred times.

Leah, Mindy, Amanda, Kendra, Barbara, Laura, Kathy, Diane— my betas. Y'all are the bomb, and y'all are awesome.

CONTENTS

The Uncertain Saints

Whiskey Neat

Jack & Coke

Vodka On The Rocks

Bad Apple

Dirty Mother

Rusty Nail

The Kilgore Fire Series

Shock Advised

Flash Point

Oxygen Deprived

Controlled Burn

Put Out

I Like Big Dragons Series

I Like Big Dragons and I Cannot Lie

Dragons Need Love, Too

Oh, My Dragon

The Dixie Warden Rejects

Beard Mode

Fear the Beard

Son of a Beard

I'm Only Here for the Beard

The Beard Made Me Do It

Beard Up

For the Love of Beard

Law & Beard (3-8-18)

There's No Crying in Baseball
Pitch Please

George's story (March of 2018)

The Hail Raisers
Hail No

Go to Hail

Burn in Hail

What the Hail

The Hail You Say

Hail Mary (2-8-18)

The Simple Man Series

Kinda Don't Care (Rafe and Janie)

PROLOGUE

I have no idea what I'm doing.
-Krisney every single day of her life

Krisney

16 years and one day ago

I closed my eyes, prayed that he'd leave, and started counting.

One.

He ran his fingers through my hair.

They were sticky.

Two.

I smelled something that was unmistakable. There was no other thing that it could be, and my stomach rolled as the sticky substance was dragged onto my face.

Three.

I would've shuddered, but then that would've let him know that I was awake, and that wouldn't end up good for me.

An eternity later, I got to one hundred, and cried when he walked out the door.

Sometimes it was like that.

There were days when he'd just come and sit, watching me squirm.

Well, at least that's what it felt like.

I had a feeling he didn't know that he woke me every time he walked into my room.

There was this sort of sixth sense that I started to have when this all started.

I couldn't begin to tell you how long it'd been going on.

A while.

I couldn't remember exactly how long, really.

It was likely happening longer than I thought, but I remember the specific date because it'd been on my birthday when he'd finally stopped watching.

I had no clue that the next day my life would totally change or that I'd fall head over heels in love with a Hail.

It was only twelve hours later when I met the boy that would change my life.

Though, it'd be another two years before I realized what he meant to me.

Two minutes after that second meeting to make me fall in love with him.

And thirty seconds after that to know that I couldn't live without him.

CHAPTER 1

What if I have a child that's allergic to dogs and I have to get rid of the child?
-Reed to his mother

Reed

16 years ago

The first time I saw her, I nearly fell out of my truck.

I remembered it like it was yesterday.

She was wearing a pale lavender top, short—and when I say short, I mean that if she bent over I'd see her underwear—khaki shorts. A pair of simple black flip flops from Old Navy—the ones that are a dollar on sale every other week—and she had her hair up in a ponytail with the length of the ponytail braided down to her bra strap.

Her long, strawberry blonde hair seemed to shimmer and shine under the street lamp, and I wanted to touch it. Wrap my fingers around the length and bring it up to my nose to smell.

We met because her best friend and my friend wanted to meet. Each of us had tagged along, neither of us realizing that we were about to have our lives changed forever.

"Come on," Drake said. "It's time to go."

I rolled my eyes and walked with my friend out to my truck. And it was my truck, because if it was his, I knew that I wouldn't get a say so in what time we left.

What if this girl was his soulmate? I didn't want to have to stay out there until dawn. I wanted to be able to go home at a normal time, because I had a baseball game the next day.

Thinking about how much this was going to suck, I drove slowly, uncaring whether Drake was bitching in the seat next to me.

"Could you drive any slower?" Drake, aka Dilbert as I liked to call him, groaned.

"I can't get another ticket," I told him honestly. "I was barely able to pay for the last one. If I get another, I have to go to teen court to get it dismissed and that would fucking blow, because then they'd make me do community service. Then I wouldn't be able to practice with the elite team on Saturday, and then…"

"I got it," Drake muttered under his breath.

I grinned.

Drake hated hearing about my practices…mostly because he wasn't as good as me and couldn't keep up with me at all.

That wasn't vanity talking, either.

I played on two club teams. One for baseball, and one for soccer. Lucky enough for me, they split the seasons. Fall and spring it was baseball. Winter and summer, soccer.

When I wasn't playing games for one, I was practicing for another.

At one point, Drake had been on the baseball team with me, but he quit shortly after his father and mother caught him trying to juice himself—or shoot himself up with steroids—to keep up with me.

Which had upset me, too.

Now we were just friends, and I made it a point to chill and relax with him, since I think the whole reason he tried was because we'd been the best of friends during our younger years, but had grown apart as we got older.

"Okay, she's going to have her friend there, so if we disappear for a little while, you have to take one for the team."

I snorted, knowing where he was going with that.

He wanted me to keep the proverbial fat chick entertained while he went for his own entertainment.

"Sure, Drake." I snorted. "I'll do that for you."

He pointed out a few more turns, and not five minutes later, I was pulling off on the side of the road next to a sweet ass yellow Chevy.

We both got out, but instead of going up to the front walk with Drake, I hung back and checked out the yellow Chevy C10 pickup truck.

It was a sixty-eight or nine short bed, and it was in mint condition.

"Her dad moved it out of the garage so he could get the Christmas tree down for her mother," a soft voice came from beside me.

I would've jumped, but my brothers had been trying to scare me since I was young enough not to fall over. I'd trained my body not to react, even when my body was going crazy on the inside.

"It's August," I pointed out.

"August fourth," she agreed.

"Then why is she getting out Christmas?"

"Laryn's parents put it out at the beginning of August because her mother is a Christmas-aholic," the girl said.

I finally gave the girl my full attention.

She was *not* a fat chick.

In fact, she was anything but fat.

She was small and skinny.

Very small.

Like a chihuahua compared to my mastiff.

I was six-foot-three inches and packed solidly with lean muscle.

One day, I'd probably resemble my father more closely than what I did today, but since I worked out often and watched what I ate, I stayed lean.

I looked like a monster next to her.

Also, I'd seen her before, of course. She was my brother's best friend's little sister.

She didn't hang out at the house with her brother, Jay, *at all*, and it was only on rare occasions that I saw her out and about with her parents.

They hated me, by the way.

Honestly, they were stuck up assholes, and the Hails were too middle class for them.

It probably didn't help that I played my 'redneck' status up when they were around, though.

Seeing her here was still a start.

When I saw her around town, she was always presentable. Most assuredly, she wasn't dressed like *that*.

She wasn't in anything overly provocative. All of the girls I knew wore short shorts.

No, she was dressed like a normal teenage girl, I guess.

But when she was with her parents it was all khaki pants and cardigan sweaters.

I didn't think I'd ever seen as much of her skin revealed as I did right then.

It was her eyes, though, that held me captive. The way the streetlight cast shadows that seemed to play over her features.

"You," she said then, finally placing how she knew me as well.

"Me," I agreed.

"What are you doing here?"

Just then Drake and her friend came walking down the driveway. The girl with two bottles of Coke in one hand, and Drake with a Coke in one hand, and a water in the other.

The water was obviously for me.

I didn't bother drinking my calories. I'd rather eat them.

And he knew that.

"Here you go," the girl said to her friend.

"Thank you, Larry," Krisney said to her friend. "Larry, this is..."

"My friend, Reed Hail," Drake finished for Krisney.

Drake probably hadn't recognized her yet, but he would.

It was only a matter of time.

It was the eyes, you see.

They were a shade of silvery light blue. Like a wolf's eyes.

On her, they looked almost eerie.

They were distinctive, that was for sure.

"Nice to meet you," Laryn aka "Larry" said to me. "I'd offer you a place to sit, but it looks like Christmas exploded inside my house, and every available surface has a box or a Santa on it."

My lips twitched.

"I'm fine outside."

And I was.

I was so used to the heat that ninety degrees with zero sunlight was heavenly to me. And when the breeze blew, signaling a pending storm on the way in, it was downright chilly to me.

But I didn't care.

Not with how Krisney sat next to me on the tailgate of my truck, laughing with her friend about something that'd happened to her brother.

"He said he was so happy to get underwear from my mom that he waved them around the room with excitement. Apparently, they hadn't had clean underwear in quite a long time." She paused. "She also sent him wet wipes, which he said he used about half of to wash a month's worth of grime off of him thirty seconds after opening them."

I snorted.

"My brother said that the remote places are like that sometimes when they're deployed," I added my two cents.

"Your brother is in the military?"

I nodded. "Marines."

Her eyes widened. "I want to go into the Navy."

I must've looked at her incredulously, because she narrowed her eyes at me.

The halo that the street light was casting on us was bright enough that I saw her left cheek twitch.

"I'm more than capable of being in the Navy."

I bit my lip to keep from saying something like, 'You'd be eaten alive.'

Instead, I kept my trap shut and continued to pepper her with questions.

"What do you want to do in the Navy?"

She shrugged. "Well, I've always wanted to be a dental hygienist."

"Who the hell always wants to be a dental hygienist?" I broke in. "That's weird."

"Well, what do you want to be?"

I shrugged. "I've always wanted to be a doctor."

"An OB/GYN?" she teased.

I burst out laughing at that.

"Why would you say that?"

"You look like a guy who would like to play with vaginas for a living," she countered.

I snickered.

"I guess that wouldn't be half bad," I admitted. "I could think of worse careers."

Our banter only continued after that.

And, six months later, our relationship was still going strong.

Her father hated me.

Her mother hated me more.

And her brother, my brother's best friend, looked at me like I was no better than dog meat.

But I loved the girl, and I had a feeling that nothing would ever change that.

Oh, how wrong I would be.

CHAPTER 2

Some people manage stress by yoga, meditation, and long walks. I manage stress by binge eating carbs, swearing, and drinking wine.
-Krisney's words of wisdom

Krisney

2 years later

It was the scream that woke me.

The scream of a mother losing her child.

I immediately got up, ran down the hallway, and instantly knew that something was wrong.

There were three police officers standing in our front foyer, and every one of them was looking at my mother with pity on their face.

"Are you sure?" my father asked, his voice rough with suppressed emotion.

"Yes, sir," the closest cop confirmed. "The other boy caught him raping his sister. From what we can tell, it was not intentional. The other kid was just trying to protect himself. Once your kid realized he'd been caught, he fought like hell to get away, which the other boy didn't let him accomplish. So he started fighting for his life, and the other boy defended himself."

"I want him in jail!" my mother screeched. "Now!"

"He's currently in police custody," the officer continued, not missing a beat at the poisonous words my mother spewed. "We will be investigating more thoroughly, but as of now, everyone is corroborating the evidence we've found. The girl has also confirmed that apparently this has been going on for years."

I made a squeak in my throat, and my hand covered my mouth.

He'd been doing it for years.

Funny, but my brother hadn't visited me like he used to every single night for the last four years.

I didn't think that was a coincidence.

Not at all.

And I felt sick to my stomach.

"She's lying!" my mother assured the cop. "The girl is a tramp. How could you think otherwise?"

I turned around and walked upstairs, straight to my bedroom, and called Reed.

He didn't answer.

I called him fifty-one times before I realized something was very wrong. I had no clue how bad it was going to get, and I certainly wasn't prepared for what happened next.

***

Six hours later, I snuck out of my parents' house and walked over to Reed's house. I was pretty sure that my mom would not appreciate me going over to the Hails' house to offer comfort.

It was five miles, and around mile marker two, it started to drizzle.

It wasn't too hard, but it was enough to soak me through by the time I'd arrived at their place.

I knocked on the door and smiled somewhat timidly at Travis when he opened the door.

He didn't smile in return, he just held the door open for me to enter.

I stepped inside and immediately saw Reed standing in the kitchen, his arms crossed over his chest.

He was so beautiful.

So strong. So captivating.

He only had to look at me to make me weak in the knees.

And today wasn't any different.

The anger on his face—seemingly directed at me—was something I'd never seen from him before, though.

It was almost as if he blamed me for my brother's misdeeds…which I guess shouldn't have been too surprising.

I thought I'd be able to convince him that I was just as disgusted by what my brother did as he was, though. That he'd give me a chance to explain…to offer my sincere apologies for the type of person that I knew my brother was.

"Reed…"

"Get out."

My mouth dropped open, and I took a step forward, completely ignoring everything that was going on around me. Which included Reed's parents, his sister, Amy, and all of his brothers, excluding Tobias.

Amy was at the kitchen counter, her arms wrapped around her tightly, looking at the sink as if there was something incredibly fascinating there that held her attention.

"I said get out."

Reed's words were furious.

He needed time.

I saw the error in my ways now.

I nodded, knowing that I'd need to try to do this some other time.

But I stopped before turning completely around and found Travis.

"Thank you."

With that, I walked out the door, unaware that I'd never be back.

CHAPTER 3

Most days I don't give a fuck. Today I don't give a motherfucking
fuck.
-Text from Krisney to Hennessy

Krisney

Six months ago

My mother was on her phone, focused solely on what she was doing, and not paying attention to me in the slightest as I opened my mouth to tell them the news.

"We're going to Mike's!" my mother suddenly declared.

I grimaced. I hated Mike's…and come to think of it, so did my mother.

But I didn't question her. I knew how she was. Knew how she would act to get her way anyway, so why bother?

There'd been one time when I'd finally had enough of a certain high-class restaurant, that I'd decided it'd be best to tell my mother that I hated everything about that restaurant. The fish. The steak. The sweet tea that was the worst sweet tea in the state of Texas.

She'd listened to me tell her how I hated it—I'd been fourteen at the time—and then had proceeded to go to that restaurant for the next week. Every single day. Sometimes twice a day.

I'd gotten the point pretty quickly after that. My mom flat out didn't give a flying fuck. She certainly didn't care when I refused to eat the dinner, and I learned the hard way that she'd let me starve.

When I'd refused to eat the first meal, she'd then told me that I wouldn't eat unless it was what she provided for me. Which began four long days of hunger hell that resulted in me eating every single piece of food off my plate when it was offered, and never again complaining after I learned that she wouldn't budge.

Instead of opening that particular can of worms, I dropped the bomb I'd been holding onto for forever. Well, forever being about a week, anyway.

I should've known this wasn't going to go over well. Should've planned for it to blow up in my face.

I guess in a way I had though, because otherwise I'd have told them a lot sooner than the day before I was set to leave.

"Mom," I swallowed thickly. "Dad, I have something to tell you."

Dad looked at me, his face a worried line of concern.

My mother, on the other hand, started to groan.

"We don't care, honey," my mother said, automatically assuming that I was trying to get out of the next social function that she demanded I attend while visiting home. "You don't get an excuse not to come on Friday night. You don't have to return to the base for another two weeks."

I licked my dry lips.

"Yeah, about that...I've been stationed in Germany. I'll be leaving in the morning."

My mother's head turned, her eyes no longer on the road, and stared at me like I'd just summoned a demon instead of telling her that I was moving to Germany.

"You what?"

I nodded quickly. "Mom, pay attention to the road."

My mother turned back to the road, but I knew I had every single bit of her attention. She might as well not have been looking at the road at all.

"Darling, be a dear and tell our daughter that she needs to talk to her boss and tell him that she can't go…"

I stopped her before she could continue.

"Mother," I pinched the bridge of my nose with barely concealed impatience. "You don't get a choice in where the Army sends me. And frankly, it's quite comical that you would think so."

My mother's beady eyes narrowed on me. "I can make a few calls."

And I knew she would.

But I'd prepared for this.

"I'm sorry, but it's done. Besides, I want to go."

She didn't say anything as she found a place to park, right next to a motorcycle that looked somewhat familiar.

But it took me a while to realize the relevance of seeing that motorcycle because she was busy shooting me death glares as she walked around the hood of the car.

"It'll be okay, honey," my father said.

I smiled, but he saw the wobble just as well as I felt it.

We both knew my mother.

She wouldn't stop. She wouldn't stop trying to run my life. And she would never let me forget that I disappointed her.

She would try every single trick in the book short of hurting me to get me to stay here, but this time, she wouldn't be successful.

No way, no how.

I was tired of being forced to do her bidding.

I was a grown-ass woman.

Thirty years old, for God's sake.

I should be able to make my own decisions without worrying about repercussions from my own mother.

"Mother, don't."

She had her phone out, and was typing furiously as she made her way to the front door, not once stopping to address me or the elephant in the room.

I swallowed a groan and followed behind her.

"Mother." I tried to get her attention once again.

She sneered at me over her shoulder as she walked into the restaurant.

I followed behind her, unsurprised when the woman at the hostess station seated us immediately.

I was also unsurprised when my mother got a great seat in the corner of the room with a great view of the fish tank, as well as immediate service by our server.

Grumbling under my breath, I took a seat in the corner, a little unsettled when my mother sat next to me, boxing me into the corner.

My father took the seat across from my mother, and immediately ordered a beer.

"Look who's here."

My eyes automatically scanned the room, and my belly clenched when I saw Tobias sitting at a table with his new girl. She was cute. They fit well together. Then there was the other man, the scary as fuck one, along with a family that had to be his wife and two kids.

And immediately I knew why my mother had picked this place, as well as why she'd chosen a parking spot that was really far away from the door instead of her usual close parking spot that would ensure that she wouldn't have to walk outside or be in the sun longer than she needed.

Dread filled my body as I stared at the couple.

Fuck. Fuck, fuck, fuck.

This was not going to be good.

This was never good.

Ever since my brother had been killed by Tobias, my mother had turned into a vindictive, petty woman who would do anything to ensure that Tobias and his family had the worst life she could possibly have a hand in providing for them.

I sat there for twenty whole minutes, waiting for it to happen.

I knew it would.

And I wasn't disappointed.

It was Tobias's girlfriend who started it all. My mother had made me aware of the new girl since he'd first been spotted with her. She'd then never stopped letting us all know how much she hated that he was happy, and Jay was 'cold and dead in the ground with no one to love.'

I knew the instant that Audrey spotted my mother that it was about to go down.

I'd been secretly looking into this girl, and I liked what I found out. She fit Tobias well, and I liked the way she made him smile.

She was also the first person I saw that Tobias really paid attention to, and I knew from the instant I saw her the first time that this was going to be it for him.

The Hail boys were all alike. Once they found the one, they didn't waste time in making sure she was known to be off limits to any other man. They'd been doing that since they were young.

Hell, a certain Hail boy had done that to me once upon a time. Once upon a time before my brother ruined everything.

Audrey had started across the restaurant toward the bathroom, and she would've made it, too. But my mother had to go and make a comment, and Audrey stopped.

"Trash doesn't belong in this establishment. Why don't you take those stupid kids and get out of here so people can enjoy their meal?"

I hadn't once heard the kids that'd been sitting at the same table with Audrey and Tobias. Tobias had been holding the kids, and they'd been quiet nearly the entire time. I'd heard maybe one gurgle from the baby, and it'd been a happy sound. One that had made me smile wide, which had immediately made me sad since I wouldn't be having any babies.

Not ever.

After the one and only disaster of a relationship I tried to have after Reed and I broke up, I knew it wouldn't be in the cards for me.

I was a sad, pathetic excuse for a human being. I was also head over heels in love with a man that I knew would never love me back. Which equaled no babies for me. At least not the old-fashioned way.

I might buy some sperm on the Internet and artificially inseminate myself with a turkey baster...*my mom would just love that!*

"What?" Audrey halted when she heard my mother's words and turned only her head to study her.

I immediately sank down in my seat, embarrassment flowing through me.

"Mom…"

My mother backhanded me so hard that I felt the reverberation all the way to my toes.

With the precarious perch I had on my chair, it also ensured that I fell backwards onto my ass from the force of her blow.

Stunned, I sat on my backside and watched the rest of the show with a dazed amazement.

"I'm sorry, but since when should I care about your opinions?" Audrey asked sweetly.

My mother turned a purple shade as she sputtered in indignation.

"That man who you're letting touch you?" my mother snarled. "He's the same man who beat my son to death with his bare hands."

Audrey's eyes turned cold.

"The son who had been raping an innocent girl who didn't deserve to have your filthy, fucked up son touching her," Audrey pointed out.

"Jay was a good person," my father bellowed.

My father was obviously trying to protect my mother…just like he always did.

Jesus Christ.

In between one breath and the next, my father was being pushed back by the big, scary man covered in tattoos. His name was Ghost, and he seriously scared the crap out of me at times.

Ghost pushed my father back until there was more than two feet of space between them, but that only made room for my mother to step in.

"He was my baby and that monster beat him to death," my mother screeched, throwing her arm out and pointing toward Tobias.

Audrey took a step forward, but there Tobias was, catching her around the waist before she could get closer to the vile woman—IE my mother.

"You think that your son didn't deserve that?" Audrey asked, deceptively calm. "Let me tell you something. Had my brother been there when *I* was raped, he would've done the exact same thing." She was shaking in anger at that point. "Then again, maybe it's okay in your book that your son raped a young girl for years. A girl around the same age as your daughter. Hell, it could've just as easily been your daughter." Audrey pointed to the side of the room.

He did.

Those words reverberated in my skull.

I felt bile rising in my throat, and what little I was able to eat over the last half hour started to churn in my belly.

Ghost grunted in approval at Audrey's words.

I felt like my eyes were bouncing everywhere, and I wasn't sure where to look or what to do.

I let my eyes flit around the room when I heard all the gasps from the other diners. It almost caused me to miss the way my mother stepped forward and tried to slap her hand across Audrey's face.

She would have, too, since Ghost was still blocking my father's path.

I, however, did not miss it.

I was up off the floor and across the space so fast that my feet tripped over each other in my haste to get there before my mother could make a mistake that she couldn't come back from. The moment I grabbed her arm, she swung. And due to my unbalanced feet, I flew with my mother's momentum.

I was a small woman. Much smaller than my father and mother.

About five-foot-one if I wore my tennis shoes, and a hundred and twenty pounds soaking wet.

Which happened to be why I went flying to the floor very ungracefully.

With her target out of her way, my mother then switched to a different objective.

She balled up her fist and let it fly.

Tobias took it. Didn't try to step out of the way. Didn't try to block it like I knew he could.

Her balled up fist hit his eye, and I knew instantly that it hurt just by the sound her fist made when it made contact with his skin.

His head didn't even rock with the hit, but I could tell that my mother was proud of herself.

"I let you have that one hit for your son, Mrs. Shaw," Tobias said very carefully. "But that will be the last one you get. Shaw—Jay," he corrected since he knew my mother hated it when he called him Shaw, "was your son. I realize that, but what you don't seem to understand is that he committed the ultimate act of violence against my sister. He did it repeatedly and right under my nose for years. I walked in on him in the act of *raping* her. Trust me when I say that he deserved what he got, and I'd never change what I did, even given the option. My sister's gone. Your son's gone. It's time for you to stop acting like a raving lunatic over something that you know can't be changed. I'm sorry that he did what he did and it led us to where we are now. I'm sorry that this happened to all of us. But it's time to stop taking it out on me when you know in your heart that you'd have done the same damn thing had you been in my situation."

My mother didn't reply, but I could tell that she wanted to.

Her angry eyes were practically brimming with accusations that she wanted to scream at him.

But luckily, Ghost saved her from looking like a fool.

"It's time to go. Cops are here."

My mother's head whipped around, and I gasped. I hadn't even realized that they were there.

Bad Krisney. You know better than that, I scolded myself.

"Ma'am, sir," said the cop, a young man who looked to be in his early twenties. "I'll be escorting you out now."

"Why not him?" my mother hissed.

The cop looked to where she was pointing. "I saw you hit him, ma'am. I've already questioned a few of the patrons about what they witnessed, and they've told me that this man only came over here to defend his girlfriend."

"He's dressed like a thug," my mother growled, gesturing toward Tobias's leather vest. "I just wanted to come eat here, and he offended me. He's in a biker gang, for Christ's sake. Who do you really want to believe here?"

"He's in a motorcycle club," Ghost corrected. "And he's a police officer. He's been one for years now, and before that he was a Navy SEAL. Trust me when I say that you're barking up the wrong tree. And don't think I didn't notice the multiple complaints you filed against him, his house, his fucking dog. I also saw you check his mail…which I might add is a federal offense."

That was news to me. I hadn't realized that she was doing that.

I wanted to beat my head against the carpeted floor underneath me.

When would she fucking learn?

It didn't, however, surprise me.

My mother viciously yanked her purse back up over her shoulder and turned around, only to turn back around and glare.

"You better be careful, Officer Hail. I hear it's bad out there for cops right now."

With that she was gone, sending a glare my way as she moved.

I could tell that she wanted me to follow, and I would…*when I felt like it.*

I was thankful as hell that I'd be leaving, though.

All of a sudden, I knew I couldn't handle it anymore. I couldn't handle her bat shit crazy self, and to be honest, I didn't want to. I wanted out of this fucking farce of a family.

My father wasn't all bad, but with the way he blindly let my mother lead him around by the balls, it was quite depressing.

He was going to go along with something stupid she did one day, and he'd be fucked right along with her.

Audrey, who'd been standing silently behind Tobias, tried to move past him, but he caught her around the waist and yanked her to his side. "Don't," he growled. "It's not worth it."

"She just threatened your life!" she cried out in indignation. "You heard that, didn't you, Officer Tooch?"

Tooch?

"I can file a complaint, but that's really all I can do. You know that."

"You just remember everything she said in case you ever get called on to be a witness," Tobias said darkly to the policeman.

Officer Tooch nodded solemnly as he turned to me. "Ma'am, can I help you up?"

He offered me his hand, but before he could even extend it all the way out, I scrambled to my feet.

My blonde curls bounced with the movement, and I offered Tobias an apologetic smile. "I'm so sorry, y'all."

He smiled at me, just like he always did. He was always so forgiving.

Dammit, my mother really sucked.

"I know that you can't control her...or him," he added. "Don't worry about it."

I grimaced. "I told them that I was transferred to a different post, and they flipped a freakin' lid. She was on a tangent before she even arrived here."

"So that was what that was all about?" he asked.

I sighed.

"I told them that while I was stationed out of the state, they needed to behave. You can obviously tell how that went."

Tobias just shook his head.

"Audrey, this is Krisney Shaw." Tobias introduced his new girl. "Krisney, this is my girlfriend, Audrey."

I held out my hand. "It's nice to meet you."

The smile that I gave Audrey was a genuine one.

Audrey took my hand hesitantly. "You're Reed's girl?"

My face flamed. I could practically feel the heat rolling off of it. "Negative, Ghost Rider."

Tobias started to laugh.

"You keep telling yourself that, girl. Let me know how it works out for you."

I grimaced. "See you in a few years."

I walked out the door to my mother's van and anger started to flow through my veins.

A new determination started to seep into my bones, and I breathed a sigh of relief later that night when I packed the final thing in my bag.

When I zipped it up and turned, it was to find my father at the door.

"You're happy."

I shrugged. "I can't deal with this anymore. She needs help. She needs to figure out that this isn't the way to go about dealing with all of this. I realize she's sad. I realize she's upset, but Dad…he was raping his sister for two years. Can you really blame him?"

My father didn't know that my brother had done some pretty creepy things to me when I was younger. He had taken that a lot farther with what he'd done to Reed's sister. He didn't know that I had been abused, and I wouldn't be telling him.

It'd break something inside of me to know that he didn't care anymore than my mom had cared when I'd told her.

So, I never told him…but maybe I should have.

Maybe if I had, I wouldn't have left things so unfinished.

And I wouldn't have felt so guilty that I didn't try to make my father see reason before I left. Because maybe if I had, I wouldn't be getting the news of my parents' deaths two days later when I arrived in Germany.

I also wouldn't be feeling like complete and utter shit and left to wonder what if.

CHAPTER 4

I'll bet gynecologists never have roast beef sandwiches for lunch.
-Meme

Krisney

Germany

Four months ago

Routine. Just routine.

Yeah, right.

I knew this was going to be bad. I knew that I was about to do one of the stupidest things in the world.

Yet, that didn't stop me from entering the infirmary.

Every year we were required to see the doctor for an annual health evaluation. Mine was due two months ago, and I'd purposefully gotten out of it.

I'd tried to get out of this one, too. However, my superior looked at me, grinned that evil grin of hers, and told me in no uncertain terms if I didn't do it, I'd be relegated to desk duty for the foreseeable future.

She knew I hated desk duty.

Talking to people wasn't my forte.

And now I was here.

Going into the one place that I knew I *shouldn't* be going.

The clinic in town was normally off limits.

The clinic near the base had an older than dirt male doctor that I was fairly sure was a pervert who kept working because he didn't get to see pussy that young anymore.

However, knowing that the old doc was off on the weekends, and Reed volunteered there for all the ladies that didn't want to risk it with the pervert doc, led me to where I was today.

Where I knew *he* was.

Shit. Damn. Fuck.

I'd gone to Germany to get away from him. He'd been assigned to the same base within a month of my arrival.

It might've been a coincidence, but I knew it probably wasn't.

He did it on purpose. Just to watch me squirm.

I swung open the glass door, waved at the secretary who I knew but whose name I couldn't remember, and signed in.

"He's running about thirty minutes behind," the secretary said as she took my information. "I'll tell the ladies that you're here, though. You can go on back. The nurse will put you in a room."

Of course he was, because the motherfucker liked to talk.

Fucker.

Asshole.

I walked back, met the nurse, and she guided me into a room.

"Here's the paper gown. You can go ahead and change here behind the screen." The nurse smiled. "The part goes in the front."

I refrained from flipping her off.

I knew which fucking part went in the front. I wasn't a dumbass.

"Thanks," I muttered.

I waited until she was completely out of the room before I changed, making sure the screen was completely covering every square inch of my body before I stripped my shirt off.

My pants went next, then my bra, and my underwear.

After slipping on the stupid gown—part in front—I folded the clothes precisely in on themselves, making sure that my underwear and bra were neatly tucked into my shirt before rolling my pants around the shirt.

I did not want him to see my underthings.

No sir-ree.

He was already going to see my breasts and vagina today. I didn't want him to see that I wore the sexy underthings for some stupid reason.

Growling to myself, I picked up my phone and blasted off a text to my best friend.

She was probably asleep, but she'd answer when she woke up.

Somebody needed to be witness to this train wreck.

Might as well be Hennessy.

Hennessy and I had been best friends for a very long time.

A long, long, long time.

We knew everything about each other.

I knew that she started her cycle every month at the beginning of the week, and she knew that I hated having tags in my underwear because they irritated my skin.

I felt like she needed to know the hell I was about to put myself through.

When she didn't immediately answer back, I started to scroll through Facebook, stopping on a picture that my other friend, Laryn, had uploaded.

I smiled at the giggling baby who had what looked like green peas smeared all over her face.

After Reed had broken up with me, I'd had a falling out with Laryn.

Hell, I'd had a falling out with nearly everybody.

Everybody was gone except Hennessy. She stayed by me despite everything.

Despite the fact that my brother had done the unthinkable. Despite the fact that my parents went out of their way to make the Hails' lives a living hell afterward. Despite the fact that my parents actively hated me because of my support of Tobias, the man who killed my brother when he caught him raping his sister.

They'd never let me forget that I'd 'betrayed the family' but I couldn't.

Not with everything that had happened *before*. And especially not with what happened after.

My phone pinged with an incoming message from Hennessy, making me smile.

It was a picture of a meme that said: I'll bet gynecologists never have roast beef sandwiches for lunch.

I burst out laughing, my eyes stinging with the hilarity of it.

See, as much as I liked Laryn, she didn't get me like Hennessy did.

Never had.

Although we'd reconnected about a year ago, it still wasn't what Hennessy and I shared.

Since we'd reconnected, I'd enjoyed seeing how she'd moved on with her life. While there I was living right where Reed had left me.

In a broken pile of Krisney that probably wouldn't ever heal again.

Which reminded me where I was at, and what I was about to do.

I grimaced.

Bad. Bad. Bad.

This was going to be so bad.

The man that I loved, the man who had dumped me, was going to be looking at my vagina.

This seriously couldn't get any worse, right? *Wrong.*

How, you ask?

The air conditioner kicked on.

There I was, in nothing but a fucking paper towel suit, and the fucking air kicks on?

Seriously?

It had to be some sort of a cosmic joke.

I could practically feel the hairs on my legs growing as goosebumps started to chase over my skin.

There wasn't an inch of my flesh that wasn't affected by the air, which happened to be about the time that Reed came in, looking down at the chart in his hands.

Without knocking.

He looked tired. A little bit pissed, and a whole lot of beautiful.

His hair was styled, but it looked like at some point he'd started to run his hand through it on the left side right next to his ear.

He had a beautiful head full of almost black hair. And I say almost because at his temples he was starting to gray.

Oh, God. That was so sexy.

I hadn't seen him except in pictures sent by Hennessy, or while stalking his Facebook, for a while now. At least two years.

He was only thirty-two years old, so it was sort of a shock to see his hair graying, but damn did he work it.

He had a pair of glasses perched on his nose, and I found myself smiling quickly. He'd always had trouble seeing when he was stressed and his eyes were fatigued.

He wasn't wearing a doctor's coat.

Why was I obsessed with that fact? Because had he been wearing a doctor's coat, it would've hidden the way his muscular arms pulled at his Polo shirt, and the way that Polo shirt fit him to perfection in all the right ways.

The shirt was tucked into his jeans, showing off his trim waist and the goddamn belt buckle I'd bought him for Christmas our first year together.

The belt buckle I'd bought him.

It'd cost me an entire year's savings from the money my mother would give me for lunch—though Reed didn't know that I wasn't the spoiled rich kid that everyone always thought I was.

At the time, Jay had gotten everything he wanted, while I, being the rebellious child who went against her parents' wishes by dating a 'bad boy,' got money for lunch every day and lunch money only. That equaled to about twenty dollars a week, for eighteen weeks. Meaning that, although I'd starved during school, it'd been worth it to get him that belt buckle and see his face light up with excitement.

I swallowed thickly and tried not to let my eyes take in the buckle, and instead focused on his face.

The same beautiful face that still haunted almost all of my sleeping and waking moments.

"Any STD concerns?"

He didn't know it was me. I was going with that. Because if he did know it was me, he wouldn't have asked.

I didn't sleep around.

Hell, it took him six months to get me to put out when *we'd* dated.

"No."

I tried not to snap. Really, I did.

But this man had a way of getting on my nerves. I could happily kick him in the balls and not feel an ounce of remorse.

Reed's head snapped up, and his eyes widened the moment the word left my mouth.

Yeah, he hadn't known it was me.

We stared at each other like two deer caught in a spotlight.

Then he broke the stare as easily as he'd ended our relationship and said, "Any concerns?"

I shook my head. "No."

He nodded his head, then looked down at the paper.

"Last menstrual cycle?"

I shrugged.

"I'm on the pill. You know how that goes. I skip the week that causes you to have a period." I paused. "Maybe six weeks ago?"

Hell, he'd been the one to suggest that I get on the pill. He'd been there with me when I'd been given the speech about them.

I still remember the doctor telling us that birth control pills weren't as effective if you didn't take them at the same time every day, and if you were on antibiotics to use alternate means of protection.

It'd been so embarrassing to have that doctor know that I was about to have sex with the man that was directly beside me at the time.

Now here we were, all these years later, and Reed was the man asking the questions. Jesus.

"Yeah," he looked down at the paper, "I do."

I winced at the biting tone.

God, he really hated me.

I knew why, but still.

"Did Dee-Dee tell you we were performing a Pap smear?"

No, she put me in this room, told me to get undressed, and then proceeded to leave me naked for forty-five minutes, not once coming to check on me.

I nodded.

She had.

Dammit.

"Would you feel more comfortable with a nurse in here?"

The mocking tone almost dared me to do it. It wouldn't stop the feelings we had for each other, though.

I shook my head no.

The only thing that would make this situation more comfortable was if I were dead.

"You know what to do."

I did.

Leaning back, I scooted to the bottom of the table until my ass almost hung off the edge.

While I did that, he pulled the stirrups out and then reached for my ankle.

The moment our skin met, I shuddered.

Which he noticed, of course. It was also hard to hide the goose bumps that pebbled my flesh the moment our skin touched, which in no way had anything to do with the air conditioning.

He let go of me like I'd burned him.

Instead of him touching my other foot, I picked my own leg up and placed my heel in the stirrup.

"It's cold in here," I murmured, lying through my teeth.

He didn't contradict my lie, only hummed something in the back of his throat that caused me to instantly stiffen.

He'd done that when we were younger. When we were together and he didn't want to say anything for fear of bursting out laughing.

"Relax."

Yeah, right.

His hand touched my ankle again, and I had to fight the urge to jerk it away.

And I wouldn't even begin to mention the way that my vagina was now practically dripping with need for him. Nope, nuh-uh, no way. It was a malfunction…had to be.

Goddammit.

There was no way he wouldn't notice.

None.

Jesus, he'd always affected me like that. Always.

It was kind of sick, really, the way he could make me melt into a puddle of goo.

Mortification was washing over me like a rising tide, and I could barely hold my head up above the humiliation.

I could feel him watching me. Could feel the way he stood, so hot and strong, between my splayed thighs.

It reminded me of the first time we'd ever had sex.

Which then caused another wash of desire to roll through me.

That had been something I'd never forget. Not ever.

"I'm going to feel for abnormalities," he said, startling me.

I didn't say anything back.

His hands moved up my legs on both sides, which I knew for a fact wasn't something that was done at the doctor's office. Especially not with the way his hand was so slow moving.

His palms were rough, and they felt like a fucking heater as they made their way from ankle to thigh.

As he moved in closer to my lady bits, my heart started to pound. The anticipation of him touching me, even in a clinical way, was enough to send a rush of need through me.

I licked my lips and tried hard not to moan.

Oh, God.

Everything inside of me was pulsing with need.

My nipples were pebbled, and I was fairly sure that my clit looked like a big red target that screamed 'touch me!'

And let's not forget the juices that I could now feel sliding down the crack of my ass.

Yes, I was a slut.

A huge, super slut, with a super slutty vagina. Slutty McSluttyone—that was me.

His hand paused at the part of my thigh and groin where the two met, and he ran his thumb over where my panties would normally reside. You know, if I were wearing any, that was.

All he touched now was the sensitive skin that used to drive me wild—and he knew it.

What was he doing to me?

There was no way he didn't know what he was doing to me. None.

His hand moved again, parting my folds with both thumbs, and I clenched my eyes and teeth shut to stop the moan from leaving my mouth.

I ground my teeth so hard that I heard them crack in protest.

Then I felt those strong shoulders of his brush against the inside of my thighs, reminding me how wide they were. How they used to feel when he would shove my legs open with them before going down on me.

Oh, God.

And that was when I opened my legs wider. Because I didn't want him touching me. Yes, that was it.

I was also Slutty Liar McSluttyone.

After he parted my sex with his thumbs, he moved his hand so that one hand was holding my pussy open at the top of my sex, the heel of his hand resting just at the top of my pubic bone, while the other went in for the kill.

At first, I didn't think he was going to do anything but insert his finger.

But when he swept his thumb down, and I felt wetness go with it, I knew he was bringing attention to the fact that I was dripping wet without actually saying a word.

I licked my lips, staying silent.

Which caused him to chuckle low in his throat.

Still, I didn't say anything.

Mainly because at this point I couldn't. I'd been holding my breath, closing my eyes, and praying that I wouldn't spontaneously orgasm and give him an even bigger head.

I should've known that I'd embarrass myself. *Should've. Known.*

Why?

Because Reed had always been *the* one. The one to make me realize that I have zero control when it comes to him.

What would've made me angry if someone else had done it? It made me happy when it came to Reed.

What made me want to cry? Yeah, Reed made me laugh.

So, something as casy as sweeping his finger across my entrance? Barely grazing my clit?

Yeah, that should've been nothing.

Yet, I still came.

It'd been a baby orgasm. Barely a blip of the radar.

But he knew my tells, just like I knew his.

The goose bumps on the back of my thighs, the way my breathing hitched, paired with the way my head rocked from side to side were enough of an indication.

And he didn't miss a single thing.

But he didn't say anything, and I didn't either.

Which put me into a false sense of complacency.

I laid back on the table, stared at the white ceiling with the panels that looked like they needed to be given a good power wash with years' worth of use in them, and waited for him to get down to it.

He inserted a finger…and that's when I realized that he wasn't wearing gloves.

Wasn't. Wearing. Gloves.

Oh, fuck.

Oh, fuck. Oh, fuck. Oh, fuck.

No, no, no.

"G-gloves," I croaked.

He cursed.

But did he remove his hand?

Hell no.

He left his finger buried deep inside of me.

Then he did the thing that they do that checks your organs from the top—actually somewhat doing his job for once.

"Everything feels good there, in case you're wondering," he murmured, pressing and palpitating whatever the hell it was that he was trying to locate.

Our eyes met then, and I realized that resistance was futile.

My knees opened, inviting him to do what he would.

He did.

He dropped his face. And licked me.

Licked my clit.

It was just one sweep of his tongue, but it was enough.

It was enough.

God, was it enough.

I clenched, my pussy pulsed and squeezed. Then I came.

Hard.

This wasn't a baby orgasm. No, this one was everything.

Twelve years of pent up, no-orgasm-having need burst out of my vagina like a rocket.

I fucking soaked his hand with my release, but everything inside of me felt so damn good that I didn't once think about embarrassment. Nor did I care where we were, or that Reed was supposed to be my god-forsaken doctor.

Nope, all I cared about was riding his fucking finger, and getting the most out of my orgasm that I could.

He must've realized this, too, because he shoved another thick finger—*when did they get so thick??*—into me and scissored them.

Oh, fuck.

"Fuck," Reed growled.

I concurred.

In fact, I probably would've said that aloud had the door not opened right then.

There was a quick knock on the door—after the door was opened—and a nurse poked her head in. "Dr. Hail?"

Reed's fingers paused their movement inside of me...almost.

He continued to curl his fingers and stroke that hidden spot inside of me. The spot only *he* had been able to find.

"Ms. Fisher, I know we've discussed before about you opening a patient's door while I'm doing their exams. For the patient's privacy, you should either enter at the beginning of the exam, or wait until I've completed it. Are we clear? I will not be repeating myself."

"Yes, sir," Ms. Fisher apologized. "I'm sorry."

"I'm sorry doesn't give the patient's dignity back," Reed snapped.

I bit my lip when Reed twirled his finger, doing something inside of me that I'd never felt before.

"Jesus," I hissed, unable to help myself.

My hips were also being held down by Reed's hand, but had he not been holding them down, they would've jerked up with that last movement.

"I...I was just trying to see what size gloves you wanted me to order for you this time," she whispered. "Do you want me to come back?"

Reed's eyes held mine for a long second, and then he looked down at where his gloveless fingers were still inserted in my pussy.

"Of course, I want you to come back. After I show Ms. Shaw out of the exam room. Now go!"

I'd have bit my lip at his anger if it'd been directed at me. The nurse? Yeah, she squeaked and closed the door hurriedly.

"You've done this before?" I gasped, unable to help myself.

His eyes came up to meet mine.

"No," his eyes went predatory. "First time."

"What about the exam?" I cleared my throat.

"We're doing it."

I would've snorted, but his fingers came out of me and went back inside. This time three fingers wide instead of two.

My hips really did come off the table that time.

We'd stopped having a medical exam, and moved into a different kind of exam ten minutes ago when he'd walked in the door. Yet, neither one of us wanted to admit it.

I, of course, was physically incapable of it, but he might've still had his wits about him.

However, my eyes were too unfocused to know for sure.

Then he touched my clit, and I was lost.

I would've screamed, did scream, but his hand muffled it—making it sound more like a muted moan that likely wasn't heard from the other side of the flimsy door.

"We need to stop," I mewled, worrying now. "This isn't right."

He laughed. That deep sexy laugh that had always gotten the better of me.

The first time I'd had sex not in the privacy of mine or Reed's bedroom, he'd given me that same laugh. The laugh that made me tingle all over while teasingly mocking me at the same time.

The last time he'd laughed at me like that, he'd had me up against a wall outside of his brother's graduation party. He'd wanted to do it in a closet with seventy of our closest family and friends on the other side. And I'd done it after a little persuasion on his part.

I'd grown up since then, though. I was a different person. I was a stronger person.

Right?

Wrong.

I'd dreamed of Reed for twelve years. I'd imagined him in every way possible since then. It was sick, really.

He'd broken up with me. I should've moved on. Should've found a way to be happy without him.

But there was a funny thing about love.

It didn't give you the choice on *who* you loved, or how much love you could give them. Seems that Reed got all of my love. I tried. I really tried to move on from the debilitating pain, yet here I lay, as if not a single heartbreaking day had gone by.

Twelve years after he broke up with me, and I still couldn't tell him no.

Because one more day with Reed, even though I knew there'd never be anything else with him, was better than no Reed at all.

I needed him like I needed to breathe. Like I craved Cadbury Easter eggs during Christmas time, and frozen Snicker bars in the dead of winter.

I'd give up bread to be with him.

"Please!"

The fevered whisper was all he needed.

He was unzipping his pants and taking his cock out of the hole in his boxers and pants seconds later.

His cock was the same. Big, thick, and beautiful. He'd always been well-endowed, and time hadn't changed that.

I bit my lip, watching him watch me, and moaned in need as I squirmed on the table.

He didn't waste time. He didn't act like this was all right.

We both knew it wasn't.

It wasn't all right, and never would be.

But we were doing it.

He pushed his cock into me. No build up. No pussy footing around. He forced himself into me, the way we both knew I liked it, and made me take him. Forced me.

He was so big. He always had been.

God, I *loved* that burning stretch. I'd missed it, and hadn't realized how much until just that moment.

"Fuck."

We'd both said the words.

We both felt them, too.

I circled my hips, hoping to urge him on, but he held my hips with both hands pressing down and forced me to stay still.

"Trying not to come," he told me.

I wasn't.

I pulsed my pussy, squeezing his member, hoping to urge him on.

It only backfired, though.

See, here's the thing.

I'd always, always been great at orgasming when it came to Reed. There'd never been one time that I could think of that I hadn't come.

Yet, coming as many times as I had today, and still coming?

That was unheard of, even for Reed.

So, when I came a third time, this time with nothing but his cock stretching me, and my pussy squeezing him, it surprised us both.

I was momentarily stunned.

He couldn't hold back.

He started to roughly take me, so hard and fast that I couldn't catch up.

One orgasm went into another, and I was begging him for something, unsure what it was.

"I need…"

He knew exactly what I needed.

One second I was on my back, my feet in the stirrups, and the next I was on my belly and yanked down.

I was short. Even with the stool at the bottom of the table pulled out, I barely touched.

And he took advantage of that—of my vulnerability.

He fucked me hard, fast, and without restraint.

His cock filled me so full that I wasn't able to do anything but take him.

His fisted hand went to the table by my head, and I turned to study it.

My entire body jolted with each of his thrusts, and they felt so good that I was nearly screaming with the intensity of my impending orgasm.

I could feel it building. Could feel the wave about to roll over me.

Which was why I latched onto his wrist with my teeth to distract myself, and offer myself a buffer to the wail that I knew was about to leave my lips.

He didn't so much as flinch.

He'd put it there on purpose, of course.

We'd done this very same thing hundreds of times over the course of our relationship.

When you were a teenager, trying to sneak your boyfriend into your room so you could do it, you had to come up with ideas to keep quiet.

That's why, almost in the very spot that I was locked onto his wrist, there was a scar of teeth prints from the very first time that we'd done it.

He'd told me to 'bite down' to keep quiet when he'd taken my virginity.

I'd done it, and then bitten him so hard that I'd broken his skin when he'd shoved his massive cock into me. It'd healed, eventually, but in its place left a scar that would forever remind him of our time together.

Of our first time together.

But I didn't break his skin this time.

I knew how hard to bite, and knew that I wouldn't hurt him. As did he.

And when I felt his thumb brush over my asshole, that was all I needed.

The orgasm that took me over would've swept me off my feet had I been using them. I was thankful for the table that was holding me up.

Knowing he'd taken care of me, he lifted one of my legs, and slowed way down.

So slow, in fact, that I realized he was trying to draw this out. Make it last longer.

But then a knock sounded at the door. "Dr. Hail, your next patient is in room 4 and she thinks she's having contractions."

Reed paused halfway inside of me. "Set her up on the monitors. I'll be through in a few moments."

Then he slammed back inside of me, completely lifting me up off the table.

My mouth opened in surprise.

And then he continued to slam inside.

Our hips met. Slap. Slap. Slap. Slap.

He needed four more strokes before he came.

Inside of me.

We both breathed heavily after he was through, and it took him at least two minutes to pull out of me.

The minute he was gone, so was the moment.

He was back to professional.

"Don't think we can get that Pap smear done," he muttered to himself. "You'll have to come back."

I snorted.

I wasn't coming back. No way, no how.

"Okay," I lied, standing up.

The minute my feet were on the ground, I felt him leaking out of me.

His eyes went down when mine did, and I watched as his release slipped down the inside of my thigh.

I caught it with my hand, and tried to scoop up the most that I could.

When my eyes met his once again, they were blazing.

Which had to be the reason I brought that come up to my mouth and licked it.

His mouth parted.

Another knock at the door.

"Sir, she's having contractions three minutes apart, and she's dilated to a five."

"Send her to the hospital," Reed barked through the door. "I'll get over there now."

And that's when the tears started to fall.

But did Reed do anything? *No.*

Did he react in any way? *Hell no.*

He just tucked his dick into his pants, drew the curtain over the door that he'd never shut to begin with, and left the room. Leaving me standing there, naked, with a handful of his come.

It really couldn't feel worse…could it?

***

An hour later, I was in my superior's office.

I closed my eyes and counted to ten.

"I need leave…"

When Coralee, my supervisor, didn't say anything for a few moments, I finally looked at her.

"Why are you here?"

I looked away.

"Why are you asking?"

"Krisney, look at me."

I didn't want to.

But it was ingrained in me to pay attention to my superiors, so I did just that despite not wanting to.

"You literally begged me to come here because you wanted to get away from them…this was only for a temporary basis, anyway, until the position could be filled…why don't you do what you've always wanted to do?"

I looked away.

"I don't…" I looked at my hands. "I don't have any reason not to anymore, do I?"

She shook her head.

"Then go. Live your life. Your parents can't ruin it anymore, can they?"

"No."

They couldn't.

They were dead.

And I was happy…wasn't I?

CHAPTER 5

Who needs a boyfriend when your bank account goes down every day?
-Text from Krisney to Hennessy

Krisney

Three months ago

"I don't understand," the realtor, Madeline, said. "You have a house."

I gritted my teeth to keep the angry comment from spewing out.

Instead, I carefully placed my hands in my lap and looked at her.

"I know that my *parents* had a house," I said carefully. "And I don't want to live there. I want to sell it. Then I want to move into *that* house."

The realtor looked at the house that was behind her, a look of utter horror on her face.

Madeline was the one and only realtor in the area who consistently made it through the years. She was good at her job, smart, intelligent, and genuinely a pretty good realtor.

As a person, though…well, let's just say that she left a lot to be desired.

She also had been a good friend of my mother's and that should be understanding enough right there.

She was part of the country club in town. She only wore the best clothes—which was odd in our small, laid back town seeing as nobody dressed up, even the doctors when they went to work. I was fairly sure that the judge wore jeans and a t-shirt under his robes half the time.

But Madeline was stuck up, and she'd always felt the same way that my parents had.

That they were better than everyone else.

Which extended to me, apparently.

"I just don't understand why you wouldn't want to live in your parents' house," she continued as if I hadn't even said anything.

I can tell you why, I mused inwardly. *Because my brother and mother's stink permeate that house, and I can't fucking breathe when I'm inside of it.*

I didn't actually say that, however. Mostly because I wanted the house behind her, and I didn't want to piss her off before I got it.

"It's just too hard to live there. I can't stop thinking about them," I told her, lying through my teeth, and making her think that it was my parents' deaths that were the reason I couldn't live there, and not the real reason.

Though, the statement was partially true.

I couldn't stay in my room anymore at that house, because the memories of what used to happen in it were enough to choke me. It also reminded me of who I didn't save from the same fate.

When I'd come back after my parents' deaths, I'd gone to the house and had placed my belongings in the maids' quarters.

That was the one room where I didn't have some sort of bad memory.

"Oh, darling girl," Madeline cooed. "We can find you someplace. Why this place specifically?"

Because this is the one place, in this whole entire town, that doesn't remind me of my parents or Jay. It reminds me of Reed.

"I like it," I answered. "I'm planning on building a new house, and this land is beautiful."

Partial truth.

The land *was* beautiful. But I wasn't going to build a new house. I was going to fix up the two-story farm house that was there and make it my home.

I'd always envisioned myself living there.

The way Reed and I had wanted to paint it a clean white. How we wanted a front porch swing we could sit on every night. How we wanted a large, open, bright kitchen with a massive island where we could both cook dinner together on.

Being gone for ten years, and only coming back for visits, I shouldn't have any sort of tie to Hostel at all. There was literally nobody but Hennessy here for me.

After arriving last month to deal with my mother and father's affairs and putting the house on the market, there was nothing left for me here.

Hennessy, though, was my best friend, and forever would be, and she had a husband now. She had other responsibilities and didn't need me.

I had nothing here. No job. No house. No family.

Nothing.

I could go anywhere in the world. Anywhere.

Yet I was here, looking at this house, because I knew that I wanted it.

That Reed and I had wanted it, way back when I was happy.

Which, if I thought about it, was the only reason I wanted it.

That was the last time I could ever truly say that I was happy.

I was chasing after my happy. Logically, I knew that buying this place wasn't going to give it to me, but it was a start.

I couldn't see myself anywhere but here.

Why?

Because, if I was being one hundred percent honest, this was where Reed was.

Not the physical Reed, but my memories of Reed.

Memories of my happy.

And that's where I wanted to be.

I just wanted to feel something…anything…besides this deep sorrow that felt like it was lodged deep in my chest.

A feeling that never felt like it was going to leave.

God.

I'd do anything to feel something besides sadness again.

Anything.

I could put on a good show, but in the end, I was still just as sad underneath the false laughs as I was when I wasn't putting on a smile.

"This place has been on the market for ten years," the realtor said.

I knew that.

"They're looking for the perfect buyers, to be honest. This place has been looked at by so many people. So many it's not even funny," she mentioned. "But they always want to meet with the prospective buyer. They always say no."

I looked Madeline straight in the face and said, "Ask them."

Forty-five minutes later, I was watching the old man with surprise.

"You're the girl that used to sneak up here."

I knew the minute he saw me that he remembered who I was.

Though, it was hard not to when a couple of teenagers used to be on your property as much as Reed and I had been. We'd swam naked in the man's pond, and ran these woods like they were our own. Sure, it'd been wrong…but Reed and I hadn't done anything truly illegal. We'd just spent time here.

I bit my lip. "Yes."

The man's smile was genuine.

"That boy still around?"

Something in my face must've showed my dismay, because his eyes closed.

"You and him…y'all reminded me so much of my Jossy," he said. "You want it?"

I nodded my head. "Yes, sir."

His eyes took me in. "You got it."

Relief like I'd never felt before poured through me.

"You really mean that?"

He grinned, showing me that he didn't have his teeth in.

I wanted to laugh, but I didn't.

"Yes, I mean it," he answered. "But, before you go walking these woods…"

I paused, looking at him. "Yeah?"

"Have someone come out and sweep it for traps…I gotta say, in my younger days once I got back from war, I wasn't in a good place." He cleared his throat. "My Jossy saved me from that. But before she came…everything made me jittery. There are a few traps set up throughout the acreage…I don't want you to get hurt walking out there by yourself."

I should've listened, but I didn't. Why? Because I thought I knew. I thought, since I'd spent so much time here, and we'd never seen anything like that around, that there couldn't possibly be anything there.

Oh, how wrong I was.

CHAPTER 6

Well aren't we just two scoops of grumpy with a dash of asshole
this morning.
-Baylor to Reed

Reed

Present

I read the scribbled note and smiled.

Just because you drive a big truck, doesn't mean that you can park
like a dick. :)

It wasn't signed, but it didn't need to be. I knew exactly who it was
from. I'd know that pretty handwriting anywhere. Krisney had
always had such pretty handwriting. Though, now, it looked a little
more elegant.

I flipped the paper over and saw a receipt for a package of Skittles,
two Dr. Peppers, and a bag of pork rinds from yesterday.

Krisney.

Though, she likely didn't know that it was my truck she was
writing that note on. Otherwise, she wouldn't have bothered.

I wanted to tell her it was hard as hell to park a dually in a fucking
parking spot made for a goddamn compact car, but then I would
have to talk to her. Then I'd have to admit to myself that I fucking
missed her.

I'd arrived in town two days prior, and I was walking into my new
job located at the county hospital. The private practice that I
accepted a position with had their offices there.

My brother, Travis, was kind of pissed that I wasn't working full-time for him like he'd hoped, but the OB position at the clinic in town had opened up suddenly and I'd pounced on it.

Not that I didn't love the auto recovery business, but I didn't like it as much as my job as an OB/GYN.

But the real excitement didn't have to do with actually being at home. Nor did it have to do with the fact that I was no longer in Germany away from my family.

Nope.

The one and only reason I was excited to be home had to do with a certain strawberry blonde with the long hair and bouncy curls. The one who had the power to bring me to my knees with just a look.

Yep, that woman was my heart and soul. A heart and soul that I couldn't have.

The night that I found out that her brother had raped my sister— and had been raping my sister for quite a long time—I had called it quits with us.

I loved her, but I wasn't sure how the hell we were going to come back from that.

I mean, how do you look a person in the face and tell her that it's okay that her brother raped your sister?

Sure, she didn't have a goddamn thing to do with it, but my mind wasn't fucking rational.

It was a swirl of emotions, and I was just trying to do the right thing.

Not to mention I knew it'd be hard for Amy to see Krisney every day and not be reminded of what had been done to her—for two fucking years. Now, it didn't matter, because Amy had committed suicide.

Goddammit.

I wiped my hand across my brow and wiped it on my slacks, wishing I could wear jeans.

And I would…eventually.

Once I was established, then I'd start wearing whatever the fuck I wanted. Until then, though, I'd make it look like I was one to follow the rules.

Which was laughable, really.

Rules were meant to be broken.

Which made me look like a hypocrite seeing as I wouldn't break my own rules when it came to Krisney.

It hurt to see her fucking handwriting.

It was more than obvious to anyone who ever saw us together, heard about us together, that we still had feelings for each other.

Growling under my breath, I got into my truck and made my around to the doctor's parking lot, trying super fucking hard not to think about what Krisney had written, or how she fucking smelled, or the way she parted her goddamn hair now.

Nope. I thought about what I was going to do when I got home— drink some beer.

I thought about what I was going to eat—cold pizza.

I even contemplated going to help Travis out once I was done here—which didn't last long because I decided I was still angry with him for telling me I was a douche bag for taking a job when I knew he needed help.

What the fuck ever.

That man had men working for him now. It wasn't my fault that he had more work than people to do it.

By the time I'd pulled into the hospital, I'd effectively thought about nothing important.

I walked inside, straight up to the office that I'd be working in, and didn't stop until I was in what they called my new office but was more like a fucking filing room with overflow filing cabinets.

The cabinets were empty, but they still were taking up the majority of the room.

There was a small desk in the corner of the room that followed the wall in an L shape.

There was a tiny postage stamp-sized window with bars on it and a paper shredder.

That was it.

Not a single thing else to make this room look anything like anything other than what it was – a medical records room.

Grimacing, I set my lunch down on the corner of the desk, shucked my leather jacket, and walked back out to the back area where the other doctor and nurses were gathered around an open box of donuts.

"Ladies," I murmured, sidling up to the edge of the desk and peering into the box. "Can I have one?"

I'd, of course, eaten breakfast.

I'd eaten a breakfast taco with sausage, egg, and cheese that my mother had made in bulk and stuffed into my freezer. But one couldn't resist donuts. It just wasn't done.

"Oh!" The nurse closest smiled and swept her hand over the box like she was doing a magic trick. "Help yourself. We have plenty."

Dr. Torres grunted. "Yes, please eat all my donuts."

I grinned at Dr. Torres.

I liked him.

I'd met him before, but with me being in and out of the city for ten years with the Army, and then the Reserves, I hadn't had time to establish any relationships in the medical community around town.

I'd met him the last time I'd been in town outside of a Waffle House. We'd helped assist a pregnant woman who went into labor while eating her breakfast, and we'd hit it off afterward.

He'd been in the Army around the time that I had, but hadn't gone into the Reserves like me, but had chosen to open his own practice.

He'd said during that time that if I ever moved home and needed a job, to call him.

I'd done so when I'd gotten home, and it just so happened that he had an opening. Which worked out fucking perfectly for me.

"What's on the agenda today?" I asked.

Dr. Torres grimaced. "About that."

My brows rose, but before Dr. Torres could expound on his cryptic statement, another answered my question.

"Do you mind taking Dr. Kemp's patients today?" the nurse that ran the office asked.

I believe her name was Pearl or Opal, but I couldn't quite remember. It'd been an old-fashioned name for a young girl, though. I did remember that.

"Sure," I agreed. "I'd love to."

And really, I would.

Because I couldn't stop thinking about *her*.

Hadn't stopped thinking about her in five freakin' months.

Every waking and sleeping moment was dedicated to her. Her pussy. The way she tasted. The way she smelled. How she felt in my hands. *On my hands.*

And I'd never admit it, but I licked my fingers clean the moment I got to my office after leaving her there, standing with my come dripping out of her.

I wasn't proud of myself.

I'd been stupid, careless and forward.

Never, never, should I have done that at work. Not only because of the moral code, as well as rules of conduct, but because now I couldn't stop fucking thinking about her.

Yet when it came to Krisney, my control was shot.

When we'd both gone to Germany, neither one of us realized that the other would be there.

We'd done everything we could to avoid each other once we did know the other was there, yet we saw each other everywhere.

Then, after everything that had happened with us that day in the exam room, she'd left without another word.

Germany and the Reserves altogether.

She'd been in the reserves like me and had only been there for a temporary assignment, but I'd thought she'd stay longer.

It surprised the ever-loving shit out of me that she hadn't.

She loved the Army.

Or at least I'd thought she had.

Maybe the Army was just her escape. Maybe, just maybe, she'd needed to get away from her parents. And once they were no longer in the picture, she had no longer had a reason to stay.

I'd certainly not given her a reason to stay, that was for sure.

Two hours later, I was in the lab looking at a few lab reports for patients when the nurse, Opal, started chatting with me while running her routine tests on a few of the patients' urine.

I was standing off to the side, with a full view of the little metal door that she kept opening and closing as she explained the process she used when she ran the tests, when I froze.

I looked straight into the eyes of the one person I thought it'd take me weeks to see again.

My mouth fell open, and my eyes slowly went down the length of her body.

Oh, shit.

CHAPTER 7

My hobbies include being difficult for no reason and ignoring texts.
-Krisney to Reed

Krisney

I moaned, stomach swirling and tilting, as I made my way out of bed.

I skipped the jeans, going straight for the yoga pants, and slipped them on.

They were tight.

Sooooo tight.

I was almost embarrassed by how tight they were.

Like, I probably looked like a busted can of biscuits at this point.

They were a size small, and it was obvious to everybody as well as to myself that I wasn't a size small anymore.

I'd gained weight…and when I said I gained weight, I meant that I gained *weight.*

Not a pound or two. Not even five. Hell, I probably would've been happy with ten.

I was at twenty pounds of weight gain since my parents had died, and yeah…that was a lie.

It was because I was in a depression.

Ever since I'd left Germany…and Reed…I'd been off.

I ate everything in sight. I'd stare longingly at the door, almost fantasizing that one day I'd see Reed on the other side of it. Then there were the dreams. Oh, God. I couldn't stop them.

I'd wake up in the middle of the night with my heart pounding and not because of anything good. Because of lots of bad.

Jay. Reed leaving me. Amy dying.

God, I couldn't freakin' think.

I couldn't breathe.

And now my pants didn't fit anymore.

Dammit!

I needed to go on a run, but the idea of running was about as appealing as having my fingernails pulled off.

I needed to stop eating food, but the idea of giving up food made me want to die a little more inside.

What I didn't need to do was think about what I was having for lunch.

But did that stop me as I tugged one of the oldest t-shirts I owned on? *No.* I still thought about hitting up Whataburger for lunch on the way home from my useless appointment.

Well, not so much useless.

Maybe.

I'd been having some weird cramping going on, and I'd mentioned it to Hennessy, along with all my weight gain, and she'd somehow convinced me that I needed to go see a gynecologist to make sure that I didn't have some form of cancer that was eating my reproductive tract.

Hennessy was a worrier.

So, I was humoring her. I'd go see the doctor, and I'd happily tell her that she was fucking crazy once I had my number one with an extra-large French fry. Oh, and the biggest fucking sweet tea that they had there. Which was big.

Oh, God.

I was getting so fat.

Moaning, I walked to the closet and picked up the first pair of socks that I could find…they had 'fuck you' stitched on them.

I loved them.

Hennessy had bought them for me at the Trades Days that was usually put on a couple of counties over from us. It was a huge garage sale type event with hundreds of vendors who came from all over to sell their goods. A lot of it was stuff I didn't need, but these socks? Yeah, I'd be going back for a few more pairs, because they were badass.

My phone rang just as I was slipping my feet into my Crocs— don't judge me, they're comfortable.

"Hello?" I murmured.

"Hi, this is Opal with Dr. Kemp's office?"

"Yeah?"

If they told me that they couldn't fit me in today, I wouldn't be upset.

"Dr. Kemp is currently delivering a baby, but we have a new doctor here that will be able to fit Dr. Kemp's patients into his schedule if you're interested," Opal from Dr. Kemp's office murmured.

I rolled my eyes, wondering if I could get away with not going and still have Mexican food with Hennessy tonight without hearing her nagging.

"Umm," I hesitated. "I guess that's fine."

"Good, I'll put you down with him. We'll see you in thirty minutes."

I rolled my eyes.

I wonder if anybody ever said no. I wanted to, but a doctor was a doctor to me. Everything was all the same. It was an uncomfortable experience, regardless of whether it was a man or a woman or if it was a doctor I knew or didn't know.

Might as well get it the hell over with.

I walked to my kitchen, looked at the dishes that I'd forgotten to do last night —or purposefully overlooked, and winced.

Yeah, I really needed to do that today. Maybe I'd have the energy to do it later.

Inwardly I laughed, because I knew that to be a lie. That was why they were piled up so high—because I just flat out didn't have the energy to do them.

I'd been temping four days a week, twelve hours a day, at the local dentist office. Added onto that was the Kids Brush project that I volunteered with the schools on Fridays, and I was downright exhausted.

Luckily, today I wouldn't be wrestling any alligators—I mean kids—to clean their teeth, because I didn't know if I could handle it.

Searching for my purse, keys, and phone took longer than it should have.

By the time I arrived at the hospital thirty minutes later, I was on the verge of being late.

So, I took the stairs instead of the elevator, and immediately regretted it when I felt the drip of sweat roll down my back and pool at the waistband of my panties.

Oh, God.

That poor man would have to smell me all sweaty.

Shit, shit, shit.

I slowed down to a walk, and made it to the fifth floor with three minutes and nine seconds to spare.

Score!

Walking into the room, I immediately groaned.

There were like, fifty pregnant women there. Okay, more like ten, but they took up a lot of room, and at least five of them brought their kids, who were running around and screaming.

Fucking wonderful.

It wasn't that I hated kids so much as I hated other peoples' kids. I was sure that I'd like my own kids…but the fact that I couldn't tell these kids to control their shit when they ran by me screaming was enough to cause me to want to scream along with them.

Closing my eyes, I tried to meditate and keep my calm, but by the time my name was called a fucking hour and twenty minutes after my appointment? Yeah, I wasn't so calm anymore.

So, call me crazy when I got into the room and my blood pressure was through the roof.

"Your blood pressure is a little high…" the nurse's aide taking my blood pressure said. "Are you feeling okay?"

"The waiting room was hot, there were about eight million screaming kids running around it, and some big man sat next to me and hogged my armrest for at least an hour of it. I'm fine, but I'm a little on edge right now," I said carefully. *Not to mention y'all made me wait for an hour and a freakin' half.*

"Ahh," she nodded. "I'm sure that's it. What brings you in today? I see that your last exam was less than six months ago."

Exam? Was that what I was calling what Reed did to me?

What I allowed him to do me?

"I've had a significant weight gain in the last three months, and I've been having continuous cramping since then, too. I've been tired, irritable, and I'm fairly sure that I have eaten everything that's in front of me as soon as it's put there," I told the girl.

She looked at me oddly, then walked me to a door that said 'bathroom.'

"There is a cup in there with your name on it. Use the moist towelette…"

I held my hand up and nodded.

"Got it."

She grinned. "Put it in the silver cabinet when you're through."

I nodded and went in there, picking up the smallest cup in the history of cups.

After cleansing myself with the towelette, I tried my best not to pee on myself as I held the cup, and then moaned when I overfilled it.

"This would be so much easier if I were a man," I muttered to myself, placing the cup on the edge of the counter and trying not to drip as I did.

And I watched in horror as the cup slipped and fell right into the sink, splashing the wall.

"Oh, fuck," I muttered, watching as my pee slid down the wall. "Dammit."

I reached for the cup, thankful that I still hadn't finished going, and filled it up again.

Well, ish.

I filled it up to the first line, which meant there was barely a half an inch in the bottom.

It'd have to be enough, because I literally didn't have any more to give.

This time, I stood up and walked it over to the cabinet with my pants and panties around my ankles, opened the door, and bent down to place the cup inside.

When I did, the other half of the door opened, and I was met with a woman's laughter as she said, "Oh, Dr. Hail, you're the funniest."

I nearly dropped my pee.

"Oh, shit."

My 'oh, shit' brought the attention from the man across the room.

His eyes automatically looked at me, through the other cups of pee in the cabinet, and his amusement was clear.

I set my cup down, then slammed the door so hard that the mirror rattled, returning back to the toilet to finish my business.

Then I decided that I was going to have to make a run for it.

Yes, that was the best course of action.

I would have to run, and I'd probably die, but I could do it.

I'd done it before.

Sure, it'd been a while since I'd run, but I had a feeling I could make it.

I washed my hands, grabbed my stuff and was out the door before I could rethink what I was about to do.

I made it to the first exam room when I was caught.

He came out of the room—what I guessed was the lab—and blocked my way with just his body.

"Can I show you to your room, Krisney?" Reed asked sweetly.

My eyes flittered around the immediate area, seeing if we had any witnesses, and I groaned.

We did.

There were two pregnant women, one on a chair getting her blood pressure taken, and another in an exam room directly across from where I was standing. There was a nurse taking the blood pressure, another at the counter filling out some paperwork, and another doctor that was standing in the doorway to the exam room with the pregnant woman in it.

They were all looking at me.

"Sure," I nearly choked. "Which one is it?"

The nurse taking the blood pressure pointed to the one that I'd already run past, and I winced.

Sighing in resignation, I turned around and hurried back to the room. He didn't follow.

My mind whirled a hundred thousand miles an hour.

Reed. Here. Doing my exam.

"If you'll take off all your clothes and place them over here, then slip into this gown, Dr. Hail should be with you in a moment."

I jumped at seeing a nurse almost directly behind me, staring at me with weirdly astute eyes.

She left then, leaving me alone in a room with nothing to do but to think.

Which I did.

Oh, God.

Reed.

Reed. Hail. Doing another exam on me…yeah, that wasn't going to work.

But what option did I have? There was *one* office in town that did the vagina stuff that I needed. One. If I wanted to go to another one, it'd be over two hours away. And just switching doctors wasn't going to work. He wouldn't let me be seen by another doctor in his office when he was there.

I knew that down to my soul.

Oh, hell no.

I got up walked to the corner of the room, and yanked the little curtain shut as I reached for my pants.

"Guess you never did figure out how to be an adult."

Everything inside of me froze except for my arm.

Reaching up, I carefully parted the curtain, walked back out with the tiny paper towel wrapped around me, and gently took a seat on the table. Then laid back like I didn't have a care in the world.

This was going to be bad. Very, very bad.

"I thought you were in Germany," I mumbled to the ceiling.

There was a freakin' light over the top of the table, shining directly down onto me…blinding me.

I continued to stare at it. Maybe if I did it long enough, I wouldn't be able to see him when he started doing things between my legs.

Maybe…but I didn't have the best luck in that department, though.

I was the unluckiest person in the world.

"Came home about three days ago. Worked with my brother for one of those days."

"I thought you were there for a year," I continued.

His hand touched my thigh. "I thought *you* were there for a year."

"Touché." I grimaced.

That was the nice thing about being in the Reserves at this point. Although I could've stayed there, I didn't have to.

I'd gotten out of the Army a while ago on a whim.

Knowing that Reed could possibly pop up anywhere was getting to the point where I was always looking over my shoulder. So, I'd gone and joined the Reserves. Unknowingly, so had Reed.

Which meant he *could* possibly follow me.

He hadn't out and out admitted that he did, but I knew it wasn't a complete coincidence that he always ended up showing where I was.

I didn't think he actually wanted to see me. I thought he truly just wanted to make sure I was okay, while still keeping his distance.

Yet, even though I knew he wasn't purposefully trying to ruin my life, he still was.

In fact, the more I thought about it, the more I realized that this really wasn't a good idea. Like, if I could choose from of a list of bad things that I'd never want to happen, having him do another vaginal exam on me was pretty damn close to the top of that list.

So, I got up and walked to the corner, shoved the curtain aside, and stepped behind it before closing it again.

He didn't interrupt me.

In fact, he waited until I was fully dressed and walking back out the door.

Reed followed closely behind.

But before I could get the door all the way open, he spun me around and pinned me to the wall.

"What are you doing here?"

He was looking at me with such concern that I wanted to vomit all over him.

Well, in all actuality, I'd wanted to vomit for a really long time now. It wasn't the act of seeing him that made me want to vomit. But now, I just wanted to do it on him, because he pissed me off.

He hadn't seen me in four months, and he felt like he could just touch me like that?

And honestly, if I wanted to fucking leave, I could leave!

"I'm fine," I snapped.

"You're fine?"

I nodded stubbornly. "I'm fine."

"Then why are you here?"

I bit my lip. "I'm out of birth control."

His eyes narrowed. "You got a six-month script for it. I remember because I was the one to sign the script."

I swallowed.

That was true.

It was also a lie on my end. I hadn't taken any birth control since we'd done the dirty in the exam room.

I didn't think I needed birth control anymore. I was literally done with men.

I'd die an old maid.

I'd decided yesterday that I was going to be an old cat lady with seventeen indoor cats.

"I lost it," I lied.

A knock was at the door, and we both moved as one to get out of the way of the swinging door.

"Here are her labs, Dr. Hail."

The same woman who'd been in the room with Dr. Hail earlier gave him a white sheet of paper.

I backed away even further so that we weren't in such close proximity, and felt a shiver course through me.

"Dr. Hail," another nurse came in on the heels of the woman leaving. "Here are her notes. She's complaining of fatigue, weight gain, and intermittent nausea."

Reed's eyes widened as he got to the point of why I was really here.

Dammit.

I couldn't quite understand what the problem with the symptoms was, but he filled me in moments later when he flipped the labs over and started to scan them.

"Pregnant."

One word. Two syllables. Instant heart attack.

Nine minutes later, I was back undressed, on my back, with my legs spread.

Only instead of Reed's dick penetrating me, this ultrasound wand was.

They tried to do a regular ultrasound over my belly, but apparently the placenta was directly over the front side of my uterus, and they couldn't see a single thing due to its position.

Which then became the reason for having him use the wand.

It felt weirdly uncomfortable, and I was trying really hard not to think about Reed inserting anything into my vagina, or the fact that I was, indeed, pregnant.

Reed hadn't said a word except to the nurse who brought the two machines into the room.

He'd made hand gestures that I had to guess what they meant, but other than that, he was very quiet about what he was doing, and feeling.

He knew, just as well as I did, that this kid was his.

And I knew he was freaking out inside.

Hell, I was freaking out inside.

"Your nurse friend wasn't very happy that you were doing this by yourself." I tried to talk about something that wasn't the obvious elephant in the room.

"No."

He'd told the nurse that I was his girlfriend and that he needed a few minutes alone with me.

The nurse's eyes had widened, because it was obvious to everyone in the office that I was something to Reed, and that Reed hadn't known anything about what was going on with me. Plus, the one nurse, Opal, had witnessed Reed going into this scary trance and watching me like I'd utterly betrayed him.

Which led us to now.

Reed sticking a probe inside of my vagina.

His eyes weren't even on my vagina, but rather the computer screen that showed him the insides of my uterus.

It took me a while to realize he'd paused.

In fact, I was going to say something more when I saw that he paused in moving the wand around my belly.

My eyes turned from the screen, to Reed, then back again.

"What are you…"

Then I saw it.

It wasn't even small enough *not* to know.

Head—big. Legs. Feet. Tiny little hands. Toes, oh God. The baby's toes were so tiny and cute that I was crying before I'd even realized what I was doing.

Then he moved the screen some more, maybe to get a better angle, and tapped a few buttons.

I watched as the screen split into two…and I was confused at first.

"What are you doing?"

He typed something on the screen. Clicked more buttons. Then moved to the second screen.

I read the first screen while he moved to the second screen. I felt him moving the wand to get a better position, but my eyes were stuck on 'Baby Hail #1.'

Number one?

What?

Then my eyes moved to the second screen, and what I read there nearly made me pass out.

If I hadn't been already lying down, my body would've hit the ground.

Because there, in bold lettering, was the second big surprise of the day: 'Baby Hail #2.'

CHAPTER 8

One does not simply explain to a pregnant woman that she is overreacting.
-Krisney to Reed

Krisney

I made it until six fifteen in the afternoon before he showed up at my door.

I knew I should've gone to the new place.

I guess I should've known that it was coming, to be honest.

But I didn't.

There I was, wearing nothing but a pair of underwear and the t-shirt I'd stolen back from Hennessy the day I got back from Germany—which also happened to be Reed's old soccer shirt from high school—when the doorbell rang.

I contemplated putting pants on, but with the way that the shirt swam on me, it covered more than a normal dress would, so I didn't hesitate answering it.

In fact, since I'd already been expecting Hennessy, I opened the door and turned before I'd even seen who was on the other side.

"Come in," I told Hennessy. "I'm job hunting."

No reply was forthcoming, and I frowned before turning around. And nearly swallowed my tongue.

Reed was standing in my living room, closing the door behind him as he watched me.

I scowled.

"What are you doing here?" I questioned him.

He didn't smile. Didn't laugh. Didn't do a damn thing but watch me.

"What?"

He didn't say anything, only came in and took a seat on the loveseat.

"It's weird being here," he admitted.

I snorted.

It was weird for me, too.

Since my parents had died, I'd moved back into my old house.

I hadn't wanted to, but until I figured out a way to sell this place since I couldn't afford the taxes on it, it would have to do.

My parents were rich, and by default since they didn't have a will, I was, too.

Yet, I refused to spend any of their money. I'd been living on my savings account since I'd moved, and I was getting dangerously low on my reserves.

If my guestimations were correct, then I'd have exactly two more months to live how I'd been living before it ran out.

And I'd already canceled all of my parents' utilities except for the ones I absolutely needed like water, electricity, and trash pickup.

All the rest of my monthly expenses, like television, Netflix— which really hurt the most—and my anime membership on Crunchy Roll and Hulu, had been canceled as of today.

With the doctor bills I was about to be accruing, I didn't see any reason to delay the inevitable.

Hence why I was getting a job.

"It is," I confirmed, uncomfortably aware that he was now looking at me instead of the house around him.

"Is that my soccer shirt?"

I nodded, crossing my arms over my chest.

I'd stripped the bra off the moment that I walked in the door.

The pants had soon followed.

The shirt I'd already been wearing at the doctor, so it shouldn't have come as a surprise that I was wearing it.

But, apparently, it was.

"I thought I lost that shirt."

I didn't reply.

"What are you doing here?" I asked as the silence stretched on.

His eyes flicked up to mine.

"I never wanted this to happen."

I didn't know what to say to that.

I hadn't either.

But it still smarted to hear him say those words.

"I'm sorry."

And honestly, I was on birth control. Really, it hadn't been my fault...or his. It'd been a joint effort, that was for sure.

As much as I had thought how we shouldn't have done what we'd done, I knew that I wouldn't have stopped it.

I'd wanted it.

Wanted him.

Had wanted him for a very, very long time.

It didn't matter that twelve years had gone by. Not one of those days passed that I didn't think about him. Didn't want him. Didn't miss him.

I started to cry.

And, for the first time in twelve very long, very exhausting years, I was back in his arms.

Everything in my world was right for the few short minutes that he held me.

***

Reed

The moment the first tear hit her face, I couldn't resist any longer.

She was carrying my baby—*my babies*.

It physically *hurt* to be in the same room with her and not touch her, and I just fucking missed her. Plain and simple. I. Fucking. Missed. Her.

I missed the way she smelled, and the way she brushed her hair. I missed the way she talked my ear off about anything she felt needed my attention, and the way she stole my t-shirts.

My favorite ones, might I add.

I remembered that specific soccer one from high school. It seriously was my favorite.

It was worn out and soft due to the many washes and wears that ensued during my senior year of high school soccer. Games. Practices. Just for the hell of it. I wore it everywhere. It was an old faded gray t-shirt with Hostel Soccer on the front and a soccer ball. There wasn't anything special about it, and it damn well wouldn't fit me anymore, but I hadn't known she'd had it.

Though, even if I had I wouldn't have taken it from her.

I wanted her to have a reminder of me.

I wanted her to think about me.

Like she did every time she got into the car she refused to sell.

Her senior year of high school I'd helped her buy a car with the money that she was able to finagle from her father, as well as the money she saved from her summer job the last summer we were together.

It was a piece of shit. But it meant something to both of us.

Which was why she kept it even though she had been able to afford a new car for a while—and had a new car now. She drove it almost as much as her new one, and that was saying something since there wasn't a promise that it would stay running the minute she left her driveway.

It was also why, every time it came into my brother's shop, it had a permanent spot just for it. It was always kept open for the next time that she'd need it. And for four years while she was away with the Army, my brother kept it in his shop, in its exact spot, and I paid for the rent.

I paid the bill, even though she protested to Travis that she didn't need the charity.

She likely didn't know that I was the one paying for the parts or the space, though, because otherwise she really would've thrown a fit and refused to bring it there anymore.

We both knew that Krisney was a woman who would refuse the help based on principle alone, which is the reason my brother kept it quiet.

And I didn't want her to do that.

I wanted to make sure she got it fixed correctly without getting shafted if she took it anywhere else.

The minute she started to cry, I couldn't stand it any longer.

I needed to have her in my arms, if only for a little bit.

So, the minute the first tear hit her cheek, I was moving from the spot I'd occupied for the last few minutes, practically dive bombing her as I scooped her into my arms, pulling her in close.

I twisted so that we were both on the couch, and she curled further into me as she let the tears flow.

Having her in my arms again? It was like nothing I could've ever dreamed up.

I still remembered our first kiss. Our first date. Our first everything.

That feeling that hits you. The one full of nervousness, anticipation, and excitement all rolled into one.

I remember that day and those feelings just like it was yesterday.

CHAPTER 9

Life is soup, and I'm a fork.
-Krisney to Reed

Reed

Then

I stared at the phone number on my phone, biting my lip as I tried to decide what to do.

I'd been contemplating texting her for three days, but I couldn't quite make myself press the send button on my Nokia phone.

"Just do it, pussy."

I looked up to find my brother, Travis, staring at me like I was the king of losers.

"What if she doesn't answer?"

"Then she doesn't answer," Travis countered. "But how will you know if you don't pony up and do it?"

I grimaced.

"Fine."

I hit send, and then had a mild heart attack while I waited for her to reply.

After the twentieth minute of just staring at my phone, I got frustrated and shoved the phone into my pocket.

"I'm heading out to the field," I said. "Do you want to come?"

I was in my third semester of classes at the local community college to get all my basics set in place so I could enter medical school in exactly two years.

I had it all planned out, and had for a very long time now.

My last two years of high school, I'd started taking dual credit classes at the local college to get me a few steps ahead of the game. My freshman year of college, I started with over thirty credits to my name, meaning that I was actually considered a junior instead of a freshman.

Now, at eighteen, I was halfway through my sophomore year, and well on my way to getting all my classes done so I could start premed. Then, after that was accomplished, I'd start medical school.

Once I was finished with medical school, I would join the Army as an officer.

I had it all mapped out, every single bit of my life.

Which was what was throwing me when it came to Krisney Shaw.

She was everything I didn't need. A distraction. A person who was well on the way to making me forget my duties, and what I wanted to make out of my life.

Did that stop me from thinking about her, though? *Hell no.*

It only made me think about her more, and I felt like a goddamn moron.

Which was why I'd contemplated sending the message in the first place.

Did I really want to start something I couldn't finish?

I kicked the ball up, bounced it off my chest, and then did a few foot drills while I contemplated what to do next.

"Hey."

My whole body froze when I heard her voice.

I hadn't realized how much I'd wanted to hear it until now.

Turning around, my eyes widened.

"You're sweaty."

She started to laugh. "I had practice. Volleyball. I got your text. I was about to text you back when I saw you up here, so I thought I'd come say hi."

I hadn't realized that she was in volleyball.

I hadn't realized she was still in high school…which made me feel incredibly awkward.

I was eighteen. Which meant I was at least two years older than her.

Her brother was one year older than her, and he was still in high school, so I suppose I should've put two and two together.

I hadn't, though.

"You're still in high school?" I blurted.

Her smile slipped. "Yeah…why? Didn't you know?"

I frowned. "Jay's still in high school. I guess I kind of thought you were the older one."

She shook her head. "Jay's eighteen months older than me, but he failed two classes last year, so he had to repeat the grade. They considered letting him graduate with summer school, but since it was math and reading, they—my parents—decided that it was best to let him repeat."

I'd actually known that. Her brother had been good friends with Tobias for a while now…a couple years, at least. I hadn't realized that they were in different grades, though.

"Oh," I said, not able to think of anything better to say.

Krisney shifted from foot to foot, and that's when I saw that she was in tight black shorts—and when I say tight, I meant that they left very little to the imagination—and a tank top that molded to her every curve.

My dick hardened behind my soccer shorts, and I dropped the ball that was under my arm to hold in front of my dick.

It was incredibly embarrassing.

"I guess I'll go…"

Before she could take even two steps, I was in front of her, stopping her forward movement.

"Go out with me," I blurted.

Her eyes widened.

"You want to go out with me?" she asked in surprise.

I nodded. "That's why I sent the text."

Her mouth tipped up into a small smile. "You said 'hey.'"

I shrugged. "If you'd have answered back, I would've followed up with 'do you want to go out to dinner.'"

She started to snicker, and then her eyes met mine.

Something flashed so fast in their depths that before I could get a gauge on what it was, it was gone.

"Sure."

And just like that, all was right with my world once again.

"Good."

"I like your shirt." She reached forward and peeled the wet fabric away from my skin. "After you wash it, can I borrow it?"

My mouth kicked up into a grin. "I don't think that it'll fit you."

I let my eyes trail up the length of her body, and she blushed bright red before laughing.

"No, but I can wear it to sleep in," she admitted. "Where do you want to go eat, and do I have time to go home and shower first?"

I nodded. "Take all the time you need." I paused. "Can I pick you up?"

Her eyes studied me for a second, and then she nodded. "Unless you want my dad bringing me to the date, I think that'll be best."

My brows furrowed. "You don't have a car?"

She shook her head. "No...my parents don't believe in cars."

"But Jay has one."

"Let me rephrase...my parents don't believe in cars for *me*."

One eyebrow cocked up at that. "That's sexist."

"That's my life. My mother makes the rules, I just follow them or pay the consequences."

I actually had met her mother once before when she was dropping Jay off for the weekend. She was a bitch. I remembered her staring at our house with a disgusted look overtaking her features before she could smooth them into a blank mask.

I'd brought it up to my brother after Jay had been picked up the next day, and Tobias had explained that Jay's parents were super rich and didn't really like it much that he was spending so much time at the Hail house.

"Will your mother be okay with me taking you out?" I finally asked.

I'd hate to find out that she wasn't.

Krisney paused, thinking it over. "Technically? Not yet. I have about four months until I'm seventeen, and officially considered an adult. Age of consent is seventeen in Texas...so if that's what you're worried about..."

Age of consent. Sex. Oh my God.

I'd thought about it before, of course. But I didn't think she'd just bring it up in a casual conversation like we were having.

"That doesn't mean that she will be okay with it..."

I bit my lip as I thought about it. "Maybe we should just get it out of the way. Are your parents home? I'll come introduce myself before we go out."

She looked like she'd rather do anything else, but reluctantly nodded her head.

"I guess that's best," she admitted. "What time?"

I looked at my watch, noticed that it was almost after four, and said, "How about seven?"

"I have to be at practice tomorrow morning by six thirty," she admitted. "We have practice early, before school. I won't be able to stay out too late. Nine at most."

"Six?"

Her smile was radiant. "That's better."

"Okay. Six it is," I replied softly.

Her eyes were bright as she offered me a small smile. "See you then."

Then she was gone, walking away without another word.

I watched her go across the entire field, then move through the gates that led to the parking lot beyond.

There, she disappeared around the side of the building and left me to my thoughts, which were rioting.

On one hand, I knew that this wasn't a good idea. Jay's parents—Krisney's parents—were fucking nuts. They were asshole rich people who thought they were better than us. It wasn't a stretch to think that they wouldn't like me. Based on her mother's face as she stared at my house, I knew that when I showed up at her door dressed in nice jeans and a collared shirt, she wouldn't think I was good enough for her daughter, either.

But I couldn't see myself not going out on this date.

It'd been three days, and I couldn't get her out of my mind.

She'd always be that 'what if' that I couldn't stop thinking about. I just knew it.

And let's not forget that she was still sixteen. Those years didn't make that much of a difference in the grand scheme of things, but for state law...yeah, that made a difference.

So, after twenty minutes of more playing around on the field, I drove home and quickly showered.

Once I was dressed in my nicest pair of jeans and my polo shirt—the only collared one I owned—I drove over to her house with ten minutes to spare.

My car was loud in her driveway, and I immediately winced.

The car that I had was loud because I'd cut the mufflers off of it a few weeks ago. I loved the way it sounded...but now, with the reverberation of it bouncing off the houses around me, I was acutely aware that it wasn't going to be approved of by her parents, either.

Shit.

I shut the car off and walked up the perfectly landscaped path straight up to the front door. Before I could think better of it, I knocked and waited, shuffling from foot to foot.

The door opened moments later, and the nervousness exploded inside of me when Krisney's father—or at least who I assumed was Krisney's father—answered the door.

His eyes took me in quickly as he asked, "Can I help you?"

I cleared my throat. "I'm here to pick Krisney up for a date."

The man's eyes narrowed. "And you are?"

"Dad, that's Reed Hail. Tobias's older brother. Jay's best friend?" Krisney appeared wearing a pair of black jeans, a white t-shirt with black lettering that said 'Hostel Volleyball' on it in big bold letters, and a pair of tennis shoes.

"Oh, you," the man said, finally taking my offered hand. "It's nice to meet you. Have her back by ten."

Then he left without another word.

Krisney came through the open door and patted my hand. "Let's go before my mother gets home. If she sees us leaving, she'll want to know a whole lot more than my father did."

"What's your father's name?" I questioned her as I stuffed my hands into my pockets.

"My dad is Ephraim, and my mother is Brenda."

I walked down the pathway with her to my ride, circled around the big beast to her side of the car, and opened the door.

She smiled at me, and I felt that smile straight in my heart.

It kicked thunderously, and I wanted nothing more than to pull her into my arms and kiss her.

She took her seat, though, and grinned up at me. "I've never been in a muscle car before."

I snorted.

"This isn't really considered a 'muscle' car," I told her. "More like a fast car, with a little more oomph than anything."

She snorted. "Yeah, whatever."

Twenty minutes later, we were seated at one of the only restaurants in the city that was open that wouldn't be packed this late at night.

Instead of sitting across from her, I sat next to her, scooting in close so she was either squished up against the wall or against me. She chose me, and we were touching from knee to shoulder. Her shoulder, not mine.

She was a tiny little thing, and though she had some muscle on her, it was more than obvious that I had quite a few pounds on her.

"How tall are you?" I questioned.

She looked up at me and narrowed her eyes. "Why?"

I shrugged. "Honestly? I'm just curious. You don't have to tell me if you don't want to."

"Five-foot-one-and-a-half."

"That half an inch is important to you?" I teased.

She blushed and looked back down at her menu before shrugging. "Yes. It really is."

"In case you're wondering, I'm six-foot-three."

She looked back up at me, and our eyes met. "I wasn't."

I snorted. "What do you like to do for fun?"

She smelled good. Really, *really* good.

It was something sweet, melon maybe? Her hair was down around her shoulders, and she'd twisted half of it up and brought it around to lay across her chest.

She kept twisting the hair around her fingers, over and over and over again.

It was downright distracting. On instinct, I reached up and caught her hand, which was nervously twisting the hair, and pulled it down into my lap and gave it a slight squeeze.

"I…" she paused. "I like to play volleyball. Sometimes I like to go to the library."

That was what she liked to do for fun?

"Really?" I asked. "You don't go to the movies? Go to the mall?"

She grimaced. "One would have to have a car and money to do those things. Neither of which I have."

I frowned, thinking about her brother.

"But your brother…"

Her brother didn't have a job, and he also had a car. What the hell?

"My mother feels that I should be staying home and focusing on my studies." She snorted. "I have straight As. I could seriously graduate right now, but it serves my purposes to do what I'm doing."

"Why?" I asked.

She looked away. "What are you getting to eat?"

"A hamburger," I answered, knowing that she didn't want to discuss what we'd been talking about any longer. "You?"

"I'm thinking chocolate cake."

My lips twitched.

"You're thinking chocolate cake?" I laughed. "What about your main course?"

She pursed her lips. "Maybe fries, too. And a strawberry shake."

I just laughed, knowing that she was being one hundred percent serious.

"Do you do this often?" I questioned, drawing a pattern on the back of her hand with my thumb.

"Do what?" She licked her lips.

"Order odd stuff for dinner," I expounded.

She shrugged. "I like ordering pancakes and French fries when we go to IHOP, but that's not all that often that I get to do that because my mother feels that I'll gain a vast amount of weight if I eat like that too often."

I didn't have anything to say to that.

"I'll gladly take you out to eat any time you want me to," I told her. "And I highly doubt that you'll put on weight like she's thinking. You're thin, active and young. Those three things are in your favor. Now, give it twenty years, and you might not have the same luxuries. But if you want to eat pancakes and French fries, then it won't affect you like she's thinking it will. At least not yet."

Her smile was wide as she laughed.

"I'm glad someone agrees with me," she admitted. "I go out and run a few miles every other day, depending on how hard of a workout I had that day. I can afford to eat the chocolate cake."

The waiter came and took our order then, and he didn't blink an eye at bringing dessert out with my meal.

And later, as I watched her enjoy her cake and strawberry shake— which she dipped her fries into—I didn't once think that she was odd.

No, I thought she was enchanting, and I couldn't wait for the next date.

CHAPTER 10

Your butt plug has a metal core.

-Things not to find out at the airport

Krisney

Honest to God, I never, ever would've worn the butt plug out to do laundry if I'd known that someone would see it.

I'd just been so horny lately.

So, so horny.

Seriously, never would I have done that.

I'd even gone as far as to look into the mirror to check. I hadn't seen a damn thing.

But I hadn't taken into account the bending over process of putting clothes into the bottom dryers.

What had I been thinking?

I could tell you what I was thinking…at the time.

My best friend, Hennessy, had tossed me a box that she'd 'accidentally' ordered off of Amazon. In this box, there'd been three 'trainer' butt plugs.

Since I was always curious by nature, I tried one…and I'd liked it.

It felt almost…nice.

So, then I'd tried the next size up and had almost died.

It'd been big…so freakin' big.

But I'd gotten it in.

And I'd known that if I hadn't worn it, stretched out my anus, I wouldn't have ever gotten up to the third one. So I'd done the dumbest thing in the world, and I'd worn it out to do laundry.

I never, not ever, saw anyone when I was doing laundry.

Never.

Except this Sunday.

This Sunday, there was someone there.

I just wasn't aware of it.

I'd gone through my entire load of clothes before I'd started in on the drying process.

Then I'd felt my phone buzz.

"Do you have something in your ass?"

I straightened up so fast that I knocked my shoulder on the dryer door.

Turning around, I got angry, instead of embarrassed like I normally would have.

Why?

Because it was the asshole. The same asshole that'd held me in his arms while I cried three days prior, gotten a page, and walked out like I wasn't pregnant with his goddamn twins.

"No," I snapped. "What do you want?"

His eyes narrowed.

I resisted the urge to blush.

I was allowed to stick things in my ass if I wanted to, dammit!

He was studying my face for signs of my lying, and I was studiously trying not to squirm under his attention.

It helped that I was getting madder at him by the second.

"I wanted to stop in when I saw your car," he gestured over his shoulder. "Why are you washing clothes here?"

He looked around like it was the most disgusting place in the world.

I sneered at him.

"Because I don't have a washer and dryer?" I stated the obvious.

Reed's eye twitched. "Why not?"

I tilted my head in confusion. "Because I don't have the money to buy them…"

"Why not?"

I knew what he was asking.

Why wouldn't I spend the money that my parents had left?

And the answer to that? It was scary.

I didn't want to spend their money. I didn't want anything to do with them.

I wanted to move, but I couldn't move until the house I'd bought was in better repair.

That meant redoing the electrical, which I'd gotten a quote for, and had nearly squawked in protest. Who the hell could afford fifteen grand after they'd just bought a house with property?

I paused, wondering why he cared. "Because I bought a house, and used almost every bit of my savings on it. I was told by my realtor that the house was old, and that I should expect repairs would be needed. When I had an inspector come out, he told me that the house needed a lot of work. The electrical needed to be completely redone. The floor is about to go out in a few places, and there isn't central heating and air. That'll come later, though."

His eyes twitched. "Then why did you buy a house that you knew needed work?"

I didn't answer.

He knew why, just as well as I did.

"Why not use your parents' washer and dryer?"

I looked at him.

"You think my parents actually did their own laundry?"

I almost laughed at that.

Reed did laugh.

"Touché."

I rolled my eyes and turned around, going back to what I was doing in the dryer. This time, I made sure to bend down to the floor instead of lean over, so he'd have to be lying on the floor to really see anything.

Something that I knew he wouldn't do, seeing as he was already looking around this place like it had cooties or something.

He was also looking at me like I'd lost my mind.

I hadn't.

I just liked it at this one.

It was far away from my parents' place, close to the new place that I'd just purchased, and honestly? It was always quiet. *Always.*

When people came into this laundromat, they never spoke to me and didn't expect me to speak to them.

And their quarter machine made me happy.

Why did it make me happy?

Because the owner wrote funny quotes on a Post-It note and taped it to the quarter machine every week.

That was it.

Once I got all of my clothes into the basket, I stood up and walked them to the table.

"Why are you doing your laundry at eleven o'clock at night?" he continued.

I looked over at him in a sideways glance as I started to fold my laundry.

"Why are you out at eleven o'clock at night?" I countered.

"I just delivered a baby," he answered.

My shoulders fell.

Shit.

I'd managed to forget I was carrying his babies.

"Do you wear those still?" He eyed the short shorts.

I showed him the waistband, and then stretched it for emphasis. "They're pretty damn stretchy, so yes. I don't own much stuff that stretches enough to allow for this."

I shimmied my waist for emphasis, and his eyes went down.

He'd been trying to stare into my eyes, but he was failing miserably.

Though, that could be because I was wearing the tight short shorts that hadn't fit last week, yet here I was, still in them. And again, one of his t-shirts. This was getting ridiculous.

However, I refused to go buy new clothes.

A, because I didn't have any money to buy them. And B, because I didn't want to admit that I was pregnant yet.

Sure, I knew logically that me ignoring the situation wasn't exactly realistic, but I couldn't help it.

I wasn't ready to deal yet.

Maybe tomorrow.

So today, I was going to act like my pants didn't fit because I was fat.

Today, I was going to act like the man standing in front of me wasn't the babies' father.

Or I would have, had Reed not brought it up.

"Do you not have any maternity clothes yet?"

I shook my head. "Nope."

Dammit.

So much for ignoring the obvious elephant—elephants—in the room.

"Why not?"

He looked down at my clearly could be really fat—could be pregnant—belly and stared.

I knew that he wanted to touch it.

I knew it.

I don't know how, but I could practically read the thoughts flashing through his brain.

"Just do it," I growled.

His eyes came back up to me, and then he dropped his hand to place it almost reverently on my belly.

Everything inside of me tensed, including my asshole—which reminded me of the butt plug still in my ass.

With Reed standing this close, I seriously couldn't think straight.

Shit.

Because now that I was reminded of what was in my backside, I realized that I wouldn't mind having something else in my backside. Something else that was attached to Reed's body, and was quite a bit larger than his fingers.

Oh, God.

Seriously.

I was this sex-crazed nympho pregnant woman who couldn't stop thinking about doing dirty things!

What the hell was wrong with me?

"You mind?"

I looked at where he was holding the shirt, and at first, I thought he wanted the shirt back, but then he started to lift it. Effectively letting me know that he wanted to lift the shirt, not have it back completely.

I shrugged, trying to act nonchalant that this man—the same man that I loved with all of my heart, and probably shouldn't—was about to touch me skin to skin without the excuse of being in a doctor's office to do it.

I swallowed hard and watched as he lifted my shirt with one hand, and reached for my belly with the other.

At this point, I was only sixteen weeks.

According to my favorite friend, Google, I wouldn't be showing much at this point if I were only pregnant with one baby. But since Reed obviously had super sperm like the rest of his kin, and had knocked me up with twins, I was exceptionally thick around the middle.

Really, what it looked like to me was that I ate a dozen donuts, every day, for the last six weeks.

As if I'd added about twenty pounds, and all of it was in my middle.

Reed seemed fascinated, though.

He was running his hand from one side of my belly to the other.

"Since you were so fit before you got pregnant, it might take a while for you to see it as an actual 'baby bump' as they call it."

It was as if he'd stepped into my head, plucking the thoughts right out of my brain.

Though, we'd always been able to do that.

The other dryer made an annoying grinding ring-like sound, and I jumped, pulling away.

My heart was hammering, and my chest fucking hurt.

It always hurt, but when Reed was this close, I literally found it hard to breathe. The realization that Reed was here, but I couldn't have him, shouldn't still suck as bad as it did.

But it did.

I freakin' missed him.

I missed everything about him.

The way he used to play soccer, and then give me sweaty hugs after. Or the way he used to hug me close before returning me to my parents' doorstep every night.

Yeah, I could think of a thousand things that I missed about him, and all thousand of those things felt like a lead weight sitting directly on top of my chest.

Ignoring the way his face seemed to fall as I pulled away, turned around, bent over, and started getting these clothes out of the dryer, too.

This was my sheet set, comforter, and mattress pad.

They'd taken about twice as long to dry as the other two loads had, and I was thankful to find them dry instead of slightly damp as they were the last ten times I'd put quarters in the machine.

I was quickly running out of quarters, and I really didn't want to have to break another twenty if I had a choice.

Unfortunately, in my haste to get away from Reed, I forgot one important thing.

I forgot all about the butt plug.

All. About. It.

His hands had a way of making me forget everything and anything. And when they were on me? Yeah, that was asking a price that I would never be able to pay.

At least until he touched my ass, his fingers probing between my cheeks.

"You do have something in your ass," he growled into my ear.

Annnnd, that's when I nearly slammed my head on the dryer in front of me in my surprise to have something touching my ass.

Someone.

Reed.

"Reed!" I moaned and turned, placing my butt against the dryer. "What the hell?"

His eyes weren't on me, though. They were on my vagina…or more accurately where my ass had once been in his line of sight only moments before.

"You have something in your ass," he whispered, his eyes coming up to meet mine.

They were on fire. Literally, his eyes were hot, and the full force of that stare was aimed at me.

And that's when I knew that I would be getting to feel Reed tonight.

That look in his eyes was one that I couldn't ignore.

"I can't…" I tried to search for the words, but came up with no other way to put them. "I'm horny. All the freakin' time."

He swallowed.

"Let me go home with you."

Was there any other answer?

"Okay."

We were fucked up. There was no other wording for it.

We weren't in the right place, neither one of us, to be doing this.

Yet we would be doing it. It didn't even matter if we wanted to at this point. There was just something about the man that I couldn't resist. Just like there'd been something about the boy, twelve years ago, that I couldn't walk away from.

It took him less than five seconds to gather up every single piece of clothing—folded and not—and shove them into my basket. It took him another three to gather up the ones he'd dropped on the floor in his haste to leave. Ten to gather both baskets and order me out the door.

And then fifteen seconds to shove them in my car.

The fifteen-minute drive to my house, though?

That was the longest drive of my life.

I'd even contemplated removing the thing from my ass before we got home, but I had a feeling that Reed wouldn't be too happy with me if I did.

So, I left it there, even though by the time I got home, I was squirming in my seat.

We didn't even make it up to my parents'—because even though I'd been living in it now for a while by myself, I still didn't count it as mine—front door before Reed was on me.

"I've wanted to fuck you right here, where your mother could catch us at any second, for what feels like a lifetime."

"What?" I gasped.

"I wanted her to see what kind of filth was tainting her daughter." He growled. "I wanted her to know, that even though she was an asshole, that she didn't break you. Or me."

I could see that.

My mother made no bones about her dislike for the Hails, Reed and Tobias in particular.

Hell, they'd even followed Tobias to his home in Alabama to continue their campaign of hate on him.

Tobias had been the one who beat their son to death for raping his sister. But Reed Hail had been the one who nearly took their daughter away from them.

If Reed hadn't dumped me, he would have.

Instead, he'd let me go, and left me to a fate that I hadn't wanted to face. Not ever.

My mother had been a sight to behold when she *wasn't* pissed. When she was pissed, though? Yeah, I wouldn't even wish my mother on anyone—even the chick at the doctor's office who blatantly had a crush on Reed.

Which sobered me slightly.

I turned around and pushed inside, forgetting in my haste to leave earlier to bother locking the door.

But it didn't matter.

This house was so far outside of town that nobody but the UPS delivery driver ever came out here.

But, apparently, Reed wasn't too happy about me leaving it unlocked, and it showed when I turned back to him.

"You left it unlocked?"

I shrugged. "Yeah."

"That's dangerous, Kris."

Kris.

He hadn't called me that in so long.

I swallowed as another surge of memories washed over me.

The first time we'd had sex was the first time he'd called me Kris.

It'd been magnificent.

The best ever.

I would remember my first time forever.

And it was obvious that he was remembering, too.

I bit my lip, trying to contain the need for him, but it was useless.

The man had a way of making me do things that I never intended to do.

We met in the entranceway, my arms going around his neck, and his going around my waist.

Then we were pressed fully to each other, mouths colliding.

This time, just like the last time in the doctor's office in Germany, I forgot about everything.

I didn't think about where I was, or what I was doing.

I only ever saw Reed.

And yes, I was celibate for all those years.

Why bother looking when you know, without a shadow of a doubt, that the man that you once had was the only one for you?

I knew, just like I was sure he did, that Reed was my one and only.

I wouldn't taint my memories of him, demeaning what we'd shared by going out and finding someone to scratch an itch.

Now, that didn't pertain to my battery-operated boyfriends—I had a lot of those over the years.

All of them were no comparison to the man currently lifting my shirt over my head.

"Wanted to bend you over her stupid Pottery Barn couch," he growled. "Make you come on her stupid quilt."

If this situation hadn't meant him taking my clothes off, and running his strong hands down my body, then I would've laughed.

But at the point I was at now, standing directly in front of him, naked as the day I was born, I couldn't find one single thing funny about this situation.

I wanted him.

More than my next breath.

"Turn around."

I shivered at the low, gruff tone.

Before I could comprehend directions—which apparently wasn't fast enough for his liking—he spun me around and forced me forward.

Directly over the quilt that still covered my mother's 'stupid Pottery Barn couch.'

And then he growled.

"Goddammit."

He'd seen the plug.

Shit, shit, shit.

I started to squirm in discomfort, wanting nothing more than to pull it out and toss it across the room.

"Why?"

I bit my lip.

"Hennessy got it for me," I whispered.

He grunted out a laugh, and then pressed his jean-clad hips against my ass, pressing hard.

I bit my lip and would've looked at him over my shoulder, but my eyes closed when I felt him press lightly on the bottom of the plug with the pad of his thumb.

"How big is the one you're wearing?" he questioned, his knuckles touching my skin as he placed his fingertips against the base and tugged lightly.

It didn't move.

My ass had clenched, keeping it inside, causing him to chuckle.

"Not very," I whispered.

Not big enough to allow you to shove your fat cock into my ass, I thought.

And his cock wasn't fat, per se, but it was thick. So fucking thick.

Even thinking about it right now, buried deep inside of me, made me shiver in anticipation.

"Hmmm," he said, this time pulling hard enough that the fat bulb in the middle of the plug slipped out of my ass.

I moaned.

There was no way to prevent it from expelling from my throat. It was a knee-jerk reaction and that reaction of mine caused a reaction from him.

He snarled something under his breath, then pressed me even harder forward.

"Going to make you come everywhere in this house," he informed me. "Fuck you so hard and long that you scream loud enough for her to hear it all the way in hell."

I knew he hated my mother.

Hell, I hated my mother.

But I couldn't even get a reply out before I felt his fingers at my entrance.

I bit my lip as he let one finger slip inside my pussy.

Normally, I would've been embarrassed by how wet I was, but with him, it wasn't the least bit surprising.

I couldn't control a damn thing around him. My reactions to him were pure, honest, and excessive.

"Goddamn, you feel so good," he growled.

Then I felt him drop to his knees.

He brushed his mouth down the inside of my thighs, trailing his tongue along the soft skin in a few places.

The anticipation was nearly killing me by the time he was at my sex.

"You smell good," he informed me. "And taste even better."

And that's when his tongue hit my pussy lips.

He wiggled it, piercing my labia with his tongue, and dragged it up before dipping into my sex.

I bit my lip, eyes crossing, as the feel of him doing something I'd been longing for him to do poured through me.

We didn't get to do this long enough before, and when we were younger, it'd never gotten close to this point. We'd always wanted to, but sometimes we were in such a hurry to get to the good part that we skipped the pre-sex escapades.

And now I was sad that I never knew the perfection of this when we were younger. Although, if I thought about it, I might be a little happy that I didn't know what I was missing, either.

"Seen thousands of vaginas in my life," he growled from between my legs. "Yours is by far the most perfect."

I couldn't reply to that, either.

Not when I felt him shove the plug back inside of me, working it in and out of my ass while his tongue moved in and out of my pussy.

I started to pant, unsure whether it was okay to come.

Whatever was building inside of my body was going to be big, and I was somewhat scared to feel the wave crash over me.

It wasn't going to be a small wave, either. It was going to be a freakin' tsunami.

He didn't stop with his attentions—the licking, sucking, and pushing—until my legs started to shake with my approaching orgasm.

When he felt that I was about to go, he replaced his tongue with his fingers, filling me up exactly how he knew I needed.

I'd always needed that extra little push, and he'd remembered.

He remembered everything.

"Oh, God." My knees quivered as my orgasm rolled over me.

Seconds later, I was crying out, burying my face into the couch cushion, and wondering why in the hell we never got to this part of sex back then.

It was fantastic.

"What the hell was that?" I panted, finally opening my eyes and looking at the man over my shoulder.

He got up off his knees and grinned.

I straightened and turned.

Licking my lips, I reached forward and wiped off his beard.

"You're gonna have to wash that," I whispered, unsure what to say.

He moved forward and caught me up in his arms.

"Where are you going?" I squeaked, unsure what to do now.

Should I tell him to put me down? Just go with it?

Before I could contemplate what to say, he walked with me into the kitchen, and sat me down on the dining room table.

The stupid China dishes, as well as the cutlery and crystal wine glasses that my mother always kept on the dining room table, clinked.

Before I could do anything, he took his arm and swept all of it further up the table.

A wine glass fell off the side and shattered on the floor, as well as one of my mother's most precious pieces of cutlery.

The stuff on the table cost more than some people made in months, yet when a plate fell off to the floor and shattered right along with the crystal wine glass, I couldn't find it in me to care.

My eyes stayed glued on the man standing in front of me now, his eyes an intense shade of blue.

So freakin' blue.

His eyes had always been captivating.

Pairing that with his black hair, and now his beard? The man was pure devastation on my heart.

"I want to shatter every single one of those plates later," he told me. "But for now, I just want to fuck you."

And that was when he placed the butt plug he'd been fucking me with in the ass up on top of one of the candelabras.

I started to giggle, but that giggle was quickly lost the moment he caught me by the hips and pulled me to rest just on the edge of the table.

I was at the perfect height.

The. Perfect. Height.

His still covered cock pressed up against my pussy, and my eyes locked with his.

"I want you."

I looked down at where his hand reached between us, for his belt, and moaned.

My belly was slightly protruding in this position, and moments after he got his belt undone, the soft leather rested against where our babies lay.

He paused, bringing his palm up and resting it there.

Slowly my eyes moved to his face, and I tilted my head in question at the emotion I saw there.

But before I could question him on it, he started to unbutton, then unzip, his pants.

I nearly moaned when I saw his bulging cock poke out of the gap in his jeans.

I did moan when he pushed everything off at once, and his cock came out and slapped against my pussy.

Automatically, I went back to my elbows and watched him down the length of my body.

Watching and waiting, I nearly quivered in anticipation.

He didn't disappoint me, either.

His eyes went up to catch mine, then he started to pump his cock in his fist.

His hand was big, sure, but his dick was big, too.

I wondered if ladies thought about how big he was when he had his fingers inside of them during an exam.

Poor things didn't know what they were missing.

It was an odd feeling, thinking about Reed's fingers being inside of other women. But I wasn't jealous.

Awed, was more like it.

He'd always had a plan, and though I'd come into his life and changed that plan up slightly, he'd still been able to accomplish his dream.

"What are you thinking about?" he growled, bringing my attention back to him.

I licked my lips and said, "You and your fingers inside of other women."

He pressed his cock to my entrance, and my eyes stayed locked to his as he began to push inside.

"Never gotten another woman pregnant before." He paused, his eyes trained on me. "Never wanted to, really. Then again, you'd have to do things like putting things besides your fingers inside other women for that to happen."

"You've been…"

I couldn't even say it.

The thought was preposterous.

"You're not the only one that hasn't had it in a while, let's say that," he admitted, pulling out his cock nearly all the way before pressing back inside.

I cleared my throat and tried to regain my composure, but all I could think about was the fact that he'd just practically admitted that he'd been celibate for twelve years just like I had.

Holy. Shit.

Was that normal?

I had tried, one and only one time, to do the deed with someone else. And the moment the man's hand had cupped my boob, and his cock had pressed against my flesh, I'd recoiled.

It'd felt so utterly wrong that I'd nearly run from the room before I was even dressed.

But hearing that Reed hadn't been whoring around, either, well…that was just fucking awesome.

I wanted to cry, but soon his cock was all the way inside of me, and my thoughts turned elsewhere.

I didn't believe him for one freakin' second…but it didn't matter. I'd never bring it up again. Never.

"You tensed up," he said, smoothing one palm down my back.

"You're lying," I whispered almost soundlessly.

He knew immediately that I didn't believe him.

"I've had other partners that I did other stuff with," he admitted. "I haven't been a monk, but I haven't had sex with anyone but you since you…left."

The relief that poured through me was uncontrollable.

"Blow job here and there. A few times I reciprocated…but my cock has only ever been inside of you since I called it off," he promised me. "It's only ever been you."

His hand spread, his fingers almost spanning the entire width of my back.

I forgot how much I liked that.

Even when he was younger, Reed had always had big hands.

"You're big," I mumbled.

He pulled out, then pushed back inside. Once. Twice. Three times. All of those times were so slow that I nearly growled at him to hurry.

Why?

Because I had zero control.

Zero. Nada. Zilch. None.

I knew, if he'd just hurry the fuck up, I'd come.

I'd come hard, too.

The next thrust he tried to give me slow, I thrust back in time with his push forward, and he went even deeper.

"Easy," he growled, coming to a complete stop. "I want to feel this."

He pulled back until he was almost out, and swept his fingers around my entrance, circling his shaft where it was piercing me…gathering wetness.

And then I felt the goddamn butt plug again.

When he had gotten it, I didn't know. But thank God that he had. It was my new best friend. I was secretly in love with an inanimate object.

Only this time, he fucked me as he fucked me…which sounded really freakin' odd, but that's what he did.

At first, I wasn't too sure about the feeling. It was odd, which made my orgasm take a back step as my body tried to decide if I liked this feeling or not.

Reed, in no way, shape, or form, was small. He was, in fact, quite large. I'd never seen anyone as big as Reed, and that was saying something since porn had been my friend these past few years as the deprivation got too much at times.

Sure, I didn't watch the donkey dick porn, but if I had to take a guess, I'd say that he would more than measure up.

But when he was fucking me, his cock in one hole, and the plug in the other, I decided that there was no way in hell I'd ever be able to take him anywhere but where the Good Lord intended him.

Reed, though? He had other plans.

At least, I didn't know them at the time.

At first, he was just fucking me. Slow and steady.

My body had come back online, and realized rather quickly that this new and odd feeling was a good one.

My orgasm started to creep back up, slow and steady.

And just before it rolled over me, he stopped.

I growled in frustration as the feelings that indicated an impending orgasm waned.

"Reed!" I whined. "God, why?"

He started to chuckle.

"I want you to sit on my lap while I fuck you." He paused. "I want to see your face and watch you when you come."

He pulled out and backed away, leaving me to find my way to the couch.

I moved, and brushed against his cock with my arm, making me lick my lips in anticipation.

I waited for him to round the couch and take a seat before I looked anxiously at his lap. At his cock that was straining upwards, filled with blood, and pulsing with each beat of his heart.

His chest had a sheen of sweat, and he was opening and closing his fists as he stared at me, waiting for me to make the move that I knew he wanted.

I took a timid step forward and moved a knee onto the couch beside his thigh.

His thigh that was still just as sculpted and honed as it'd been twelve years ago—if not bigger.

Once I had my balance, I swung my other leg over his lap, all the while trying not to make eye contact with him.

That worked for about twenty seconds as I tried to put him inside of me myself—which I'd never really been successful doing. It was something about the position, as well as my shorter arms and legs, but I couldn't get up on my knees and reach his cock, as well as guide it into me.

I'd literally tried, and it was awkward.

Reed had always had to do it for me, and this time was no different.

But once he was inside of me, and I was left with nothing to do but stare at his collarbone and ride him, he stilled my hips.

"Look at me."

I didn't want to.

This was a really intimate position for me.

It'd been the closest we'd actually been since he'd left me...

That time with him in the exam room, he'd been standing between my legs, with me on my back. We hadn't been this close—face to face—where he could see every single bit of what I was feeling only by looking into my eyes.

He'd held me, sure...but for Reed and me, it'd always been our eyes.

I could relay a thought, or a feeling, just by looking at him.

He knew me, and I knew him, so freakin' well, that literally all I had to do was look at him during a conversation with another person and he'd know exactly what I wanted.

So, by bringing my eyes up to his, I knew that he'd see everything.

My every thought and feeling. My wants and needs.

I wasn't sure I was ready.

But Reed didn't let me move again until I'd brought my eyes to his.

"There she is," he grated.

I wanted to look away.

I would have...but the minute his gaze caught mine, I was frozen.

I couldn't do a damn thing but stare.

"Ride me," he ordered.

I tensed my thighs and pushed up, letting my body weight do the work as I slid back down on him.

My mouth opened in surprise.

This...this wasn't like it used to be.

Every time I moved, he hit something inside of me that was causing my entire body to break out in shivers.

"What's that look for?" he asked, smoothing his hand up my side, curling it around so he could cup the side of my neck.

"It feels...different," I admitted. "Not bad...more intense, maybe."

His eyes searched mine to make sure that I was telling him the full truth, and his mouth turned up in a grin.

"Pregnancy makes a lot of difference in this case," he admitted. "The blood flow that's already directed to your midsection makes everything else, even intercourse, more intense."

I blinked. "It does?"

He nodded, then pulled me even closer until my lips were only inches away from his.

"Yeah," he promised. "Doctor, remember?"

Then he kissed me, making me forget to move my hips.

He helped me move by using his other hand to urge my hips to move, but instead of pulling up off of him, I circled my hips and ground into him, making me cry out in surprised excitement.

God, that felt good!

So, I did it again, and again, and again.

I would've kept doing it, too, had he not started to push upward on the butt plug still in my ass, reminding me that it was there.

I knew he wanted to move it, and in order to do that I had to lift my hips.

So, I did, for him.

He held onto the base of the plug as I lifted off of him. Each time I pulled away, the plug as well as Reed's cock would leave me. When I went back down, it'd return, filling me so full that it was nearly impossible to not feel excited by it.

I repeated the move, over and over again, until Reed stilled my hips.

"I want to fuck your ass."

I froze with his cock half in, half out of me.

"Reed…" my hesitancy was palpable.

"It's safe," he promised. "And we'll take it slow."

I was shaking my head, at the same time I lifted my hips.

He fell out from inside of me and smacked against his stomach, making a wet slapping sound when he did.

The plug went too, somewhere on the floor if the thump from behind me was correct, and I shivered.

He moved his hand in between my legs.

"Normally I wouldn't do this without lube," he said. "But you're so wet, and my cock is covered with you. Pretty sure you'll be just fine."

I bit my lip.

I wanted to ask him if he'd ever done this before, but again, that was a road I'd rather stay off of if at all possible.

I didn't want to hear the real answer, and Reed would tell me the truth.

Sometimes it was easier to assume rather than *know* that he did.

His hand went around my hip as he guided his cock to sit straight up, and then he pressed lightly on my hip.

"Sit down slowly," he urged.

I did, stopping when I felt him at my entrance.

"There's another plug size!" I cried out.

He started to laugh, and hearing that sound, coming from this man's mouth, was fucking amazing.

It'd been so long since I'd heard him laugh that I literally forgot what I was about to do for a short second.

God, his laugh had always been beautiful.

Now, it was a little deeper and huskier, but it was still heart-stoppingly amazing.

I lowered myself down even further, and this time, I kept my gaze directly on his, pausing when I felt him start making his way inside.

The feeling, though it didn't hurt, wasn't something I'd never get comfortable with.

Overwhelming was more along the lines.

"Breathe," he whispered. "And push me out."

My brows furrowed, but I did as he said, and froze when I felt him breach me even further.

And *that* hurt.

Not badly, but I definitely felt more than pressure.

I was so focused on the way it felt that I wasn't prepared for him to touch my clit.

When he did, my entire body jolted, and I sank even further down onto his shaft.

Little tiny lights danced in my vision, and I came.

Everything locked down tight.

My vagina. My tight asshole. My jaw.

I cried out through my clenched teeth, and sank the rest of the way down on his cock.

One long, slow, languid glide.

"Fuck!"

I must've done it too fast, because the next thing I knew, he was coming.

I could feel his dick twitching inside of me as he filled me with his come, but I was too busy dying my own tiny little death to care about his.

My legs shook.

"Oh, God," I breathed, reaching down and pushing his finger away from my clit. "Too much."

And then I collapsed onto his chest, panting and spent, as I tried to figure out what in the hell had just happened.

***

Later—hours later—Reed got a page.

He didn't make any promises as he climbed out of my bed, and I didn't ask for any.

We'd always been like this—allowed our feelings to take center stage.

It was more than obvious to both of us that the feelings we had for each other had never been in question.

We still wanted each other. Me, though? I still loved him.

I'd tried forgetting. I'd tried ignoring. I'd tried dating.

Nothing, and I do mean nothing, worked.

I knew that I'd go to sleep and dream about him. It never failed. Never.

He *was* my dreams.

Luckily, I wasn't the only one dreaming.

CHAPTER 11

Life would be easier if I could mark people as spam.
-Reed's secret thoughts

Reed

I never set out to have sex with her that day.

Honestly, we were just enjoying being together when it sort of just happened.

I'd gotten my apartment using the grant money I'd been awarded, and paid the six-month lease in full just that day.

There was a bed in the bedroom. A nightstand with one lamp, and a suitcase in the corner of the room.

There were leftovers from my parents' house in the fridge and that was it.

This was the first time in six months that we'd actually had time alone where there wasn't someone else in the house outside of our own four walls.

"Pizza sound good to you?" she asked, sounding excited.

I grinned and picked up the phone, placing an order for a large pizza before going back to find her on the couch.

She was bouncing on the cushion, looking at me excitedly.

"I don't even know what to do with myself," she whispered. "What do we do now?"

I took the seat next to her and turned, pulling her into my lap.

She came willingly, her smile brilliant.

"Now…I don't know. I don't have cable yet, and honestly, I'm not so sure that I can hack it," I admitted. "After I get my next paycheck, I'll have to see what's left once I buy all the shit I need for this place."

She nodded.

"Your mom gave you some towels and dishes, though, right?" she looked around worriedly.

I nodded.

"Well…" she paused. "I don't know what to do either."

Then she dropped her lips to mine.

One thing led to another, and soon I found her breast in the palm of my hand.

My thumb swept over the nipple, and the hiss she let out was enough to make my dick harder than a rock.

I'd had sex before, of course.

But it'd never felt like this—and I wasn't even doing anything yet.

I was shaking. Literally shaking.

I kept telling myself that I'd done this before, but for some reason this felt like so much more.

"Are you sure?" I rasped, pulling back long enough to see into her eyes.

She looked just as caught up as I was in what we were doing.

She nodded. "Very sure."

I swallowed despite the dry throat, and motioned for her to stand.

"Let's do this in our bed."

"Our bed?"

She smiled at that, and I couldn't help the return smile as she stood.

And when we were in the bed, her sprawled out on it, legs slightly parted, I finally realized that this woman was the woman I was going to spend the rest of my life with.

We may be young, but I knew exactly what I wanted. Her.

That wasn't going to change.

Not today, tomorrow, or fifteen years from now.

She was the greatest thing that ever happened to me.

And, as I smoothed a condom down over my cock and crawled up between her legs, I wasn't scared.

Something so perfect could never end, could it?

***

I woke from the dream with a start.

I was sitting up straight in bed, and my eyes were locked on the wall beyond me.

There was a picture of Krisney on my nightstand. And beside that was a grainy photo of the ultrasound labeling the tiny forms of Hail #1 and Hail #2.

I swallowed hard and closed my eyes, willing my heart to slow.

It was hammering, just like that time in my dream, too.

I swallowed bile.

I'd been so fucking wrong.

Not about the loving her part, but about it ending.

The girl had grown into a beautiful woman, and my love for her hadn't ended. I still had the same old feelings for her now that I did all those years ago, and I always would.

But every time I tried to take that step in her direction, guilt riddled me.

My sister wasn't alive anymore. She wasn't alive because of Krisney's brother. She'd taken her own life because she couldn't live with what he'd done to her.

Could I do that to her?

No.

Everything was still the same.

I loved her, but I couldn't be with her. It would be like a slap in the face to my sister—my parents.

My mom and dad didn't have a thing to say about the path I'd taken in my life.

They'd let me make my own mistakes just as they'd done with my brothers.

Honestly, they might not have ever said anything when it came to Krisney and me being together. Neither would my brothers. But I didn't want any of them to inadvertently take anything out on Krisney. I didn't want her to ever feel like she wasn't wanted.

I laughed harshly at that thought because wasn't that exactly what I was doing to her?

I may not be saying the words to her, but I was practically throwing them at her each time I left her and her bed. Or her altogether.

Stomach tight with disgust, I rolled out of my empty bed and walked into my kitchen.

The apartment I was in was much like the one I'd had when I'd first gotten together with Krisney.

I had a plate, fork, cup and a knife to eat with. I had one towel. A bed and a nightstand with a lamp on it.

At this point, that was pretty much it.

I'd lived light through my years in the Army. Most of that time I'd lived out of a single sack, not caring in the least that I had to keep my possessions light.

Now, I just plain didn't care what I had. Mostly because what I had now didn't matter if I didn't have Krisney.

Slamming the coffee pot lid closed a little harder than needed, I stalked back to the bedroom and threw on a pair of old jeans and a t-shirt.

Today I'd be picking up a shift with Hail Auto Recovery since quite a few of them were sick with a random case of the stomach bug.

I just hoped I didn't get it.

I hated throwing up. I turned into a different person when I threw up.

I'd gotten drunk once and only once, mostly because of the hangover I'd had afterward. Nausea didn't agree with me.

Which was kind of hypocritical seeing as I worked with pregnant women all day. Pregnant women who were nauseous—and throwing up—a lot of the time.

Krisney. Had she been nauseous? She hadn't said she was. Fuck, I hope she wasn't.

Though, it was very likely that she had been at some point.

She was pregnant with twins. The hormones that caused the nausea in the first place were doubled.

Fuck, I really hoped she wasn't sick. I hated seeing her hurt. She'd gotten the stomach bug one time while we'd been together, and seeing her throwing up while I was powerless to do anything was honestly quite debilitating.

Which, if I were being truthful, had been one of the reasons why I'd ultimately left the night before. I didn't actually have to go in. I'd gotten a call saying a patient was going to the hospital for what she suspected were contractions, but I'd known better. She was a first-time pregnant woman, only thirty-seven weeks, and it likely was that she was only having Braxton Hicks contractions.

I didn't need to leave.

I could've waited to hear…but I'd taken the chicken shit way out and left while I had a good excuse.

Now, I was fucking regretting it.

I hadn't gotten another call that night.

I'd lain in bed for hours looking at the ceiling fan spin.

All the while, I'd thought of nothing but her.

And when my brother had called around three to ask if I was willing to work for a couple of hours today, I'd agreed.

Now, I was headed out to pick up a tow truck, and I tried really hard not to think about the fact that I'd left a pregnant woman— pregnant with my babies—home alone in a house I knew she hated because I was the biggest coward in the world.

I was scared to get close again.

I was scared that I wouldn't be able to walk away a second time.

The four or so hours that I worked—seeing as it was Saturday— were uneventful. I'd picked up my share of cars over my time after having being roped in by my brothers, Dante and Travis.

It'd never really been my passion, though, like it was theirs.

Me, I was more interested in studying.

Which I did. Hard.

When I no longer had Krisney around to pull my attention away from my studies, I didn't do anything that didn't revolve around having my nose stuck in a book. Once I'd graduated with my MD, I'd joined the Army, and then I was never home, except for rare occasions while on leave.

During those visits, I'd gotten my hands dirty with them.

But once I'd realized that being with them also meant the possibility of seeing people who would look at me like I'd kicked their puppy, I'd started going to Tobias's place in Alabama. But being in Alabama also meant that there was a possibility that I'd see Krisney.

Which I did.

More than I was willing to admit to since I'd been a fucking stalker.

And speaking of the devil...

My eyes hit on somebody broken down on the side of the road.

I'd just dropped off a repo for the new bank two towns over, and I was on the main road heading back into town, when I saw her.

She was on the side of the road, her lemon of a car directly behind where she sat leaning against the car's hood.

I pulled up in front of her, nose-to-nose with her car, and got out.

Her expression was pleasant and eyes welcoming—until she realized that it was me getting out of the truck.

I saw the moment that her eyes closed down, and a frown formed on her face.

"What are you doing in that?" She narrowed her eyes.

Amusement lit my insides as I rounded the hood.

My eyes scanned the street, automatically assessing what was around us.

We weren't in the middle of town, but it might as well have been.

There was the Taco Shop to the right of where Krisney's car was broken down and to the left was the fucking bank. Two storefronts down from that was the farmers market. One down from that was the feed store.

Every single place had at least four people out front talking.

"Couldn't have found a better place to break down?" I asked, ignoring her question.

Krisney shrugged. "I have no control over where I break down, Reed."

She sounded angry, and I had to fight the smile that was threatening to break loose.

I loved it when she was mad.

She was like a little spitfire, and I fucking loved it.

Maybe a little too much for a man that was supposed to be staying away from her.

Did that stop me from walking up to her and pressing my hand to her belly?

No.

But when I did that, I hadn't been thinking about all the people who were staring at us.

I'd only been thinking that I wanted to fucking touch her.

So, I did.

"You doing okay?" I asked.

It was ninety-five degrees out at two in the afternoon. She was sweating, and her face was hot. So sue me for wanting to check to make sure she was okay.

She pressed her hand on top of mine and nodded. "Yeah, I'm fine. Just annoyed."

I snorted.

"I think it's time to trade 'er in." I smoothed my hand over her belly. "You won't be by yourself much longer, and it'd fucking suck if you broke down further away from town without any way to get a hold of us."

She grimaced. "I have a car…"

She did. But it was a tiny little thing that wasn't much bigger than the one she had.

"Yeah," I agreed. "But when you need to get a double stroller, as well as all the other baby shit that you'll have to carry around in there, you're going to want something bigger than that little hatchback."

Krisney sighed. "Shit."

I snorted and pressed lightly on her belly before backing away and rounding the hood of the car.

"What's it doing this time?"

"That overheating thing it always does." she sighed. "I was going to give it twenty minutes and then try again. It's been fifteen."

I nodded and walked to the car, leaning in the window and turning the car's ignition on so I could see the temp. "Did Travis have the radiator replaced while you were back in town last?"

She shook her head.

"No. The last time I had it replaced was when we were in Alabama. The mechanic there was the one that Tobias recommended."

I nodded and turned the car back off.

"Come with me, and we'll get something to eat while we wait."

She tilted her head. "Five minutes…"

"Still reading too hot. It's gonna take longer than five minutes. And the Taco Shop is right there. I've been dying to try it."

She pursed her lips.

"Fine."

I grinned and rounded the side of the truck, opening the door for her and watching as she climbed in.

She did, and I shut the door and rounded the truck, retracing my steps.

Once I was in the seat, I drove about two hundred feet and pulled into the parking lot of the Taco Shop.

"I've been meaning to ask," I said.

Her brows went up. "What?"

"Did you sell the house that your parents had in Alabama?" I paused. "Or is it just sitting there like this one?"

"I'm currently using this one." She pointed out.

"You're currently using the living room only because you need to answer the door, the kitchen to make microwaved meals, and the maid's quarters," I countered.

She winced. "I…yes. I sold that one."

"Really?"

She nodded. "Well…kind of."

"What does kind of mean?"

"It kind of means that I rented it out to a friend that I met while I was there, and she's taking care of it for me until I can figure out what to do with it." She paused. "Your brother's club president...Big Papa?"

I nodded.

"He's going to help my friend take care of it, too. She's gonna need the help."

I could imagine. The house the Shaws had while they were there was just as massive as the one here.

"What else?"

I could sense that she was trying to decide whether to say anything or not.

Almost as if she were bashful or something.

Then she went and blushed a million shades of red, and I realized that she was, in fact, hiding something.

I grinned. "Come on, tell me."

She shrugged. "So, my friend." She paused. "God, this is embarrassing, but my friend has a crush on Steel Cross."

"Who's Steel Cross?" I was confused.

"Big Papa is Steel Cross. But, Winnie only knows him as Steel Cross."

My brows lifted. "What kind of name is Steel Cross?" I laughed. "That fits him well, I would say."

Steel Cross, otherwise known as Big Papa, the president of my brother's motorcycle club, The Dixie Wardens—Alabama Chapter.

He was a big, hardened cop to boot.

He could rival any boot camp instructor I'd ever met. He had an adult son, and honestly, didn't look anywhere near fifty—which I knew he was pushing.

His son was thirty-two, and they looked more like brothers than they did father and son.

"How old is this Winnie?" I asked, opening the door to the Taco Shop.

Everything inside quieted as we entered, but I chose to ignore everyone and instead placed my hand on Krisney's back to urge her further inside.

"She's young…thirtyish."

"That's not young," I groaned. "I'm thirty-two. That's the same age as me."

"Yeah, but she's almost twenty years younger than Big Papa."

Well, when she put it like that…

"And you think they're going to get together?"

She shrugged, but for the first time in a while, I saw a smile on her face that wasn't false. "I think that she has a good chance…plus she has a little boy and a teenaged girl that just might tip the scales in her favor."

And, as I watched her face and listened to her talk about her friend over lunch, I realized that staying away from the woman was going to be impossible.

It was getting harder to do with every passing minute.

***

Three hours later, despite promising myself that I wasn't going to do anything or go see her, I drove to her place.

I didn't stop at her driveway like I'd intended to.

No, me being the dumbass glutton for punishment that I was, I pulled into her driveway and got out.

My eyes automatically took in her parents' place.

It was always so grand that I didn't want to step off the path in fear I'd hurt the grass.

But now, there were weeds in her mother's precious garden. The grass was overly long. There were newspapers in the driveway.

Her mother would've literally died.

I smiled as I continued up the front walk. Time to see what else I could fuck her on that her mother loved.

CHAPTER 12

No one is more full of shit than a parent who just uttered the word
'maybe.'
-Fact of Life

Krisney

I was an emotional mess.

Reed had left over an hour ago, but nothing had been settled. Nothing had been decided. Hell, the subject of our future hadn't even come up. We were literally at the exact same point that we were before any of this started, except that I was now pregnant with twins.

Sure, we were having regular sex.

We'd been seeing each other a lot, but most of that time was spent with him inside me, not talking in the least.

The one and only time I'd had the courage to ask him what was going on with us, he'd looked so conflicted that I didn't bring it up again.

But his words that day had felt like they were torn straight from his heart.

"I can't do that to them," he'd whispered all those years ago. *"To her."*

And he had been right. No matter what, I knew that seeing me would dredge up old memories for his family. They may say that it didn't, but they'd be lying.

I was a constant reminder of what they lost. And even worse, I was all that was left of the person who had caused their family so much grief. I may not have personally had anything to do with what my brother did to Reed's sister, but I was the only one left they could blame, and I was sure that they did.

It was my brother's horrific actions that took something precious from the Hail family. Reed, Dante, Travis, Finley, all of them, including his parents. Jay's sins were mine as his sister, even though I may not have been the one sneaking into Amy's room at night.

It might as well have.

I was riddled with guilt. Some days, it felt like it was eating me alive. Burning me up inside and slowly killing something inside of me.

I'd tried to leave once before. Tried to get out of here and not look back.

That'd been my reasoning for wanting to join the Navy. It'd also been my reasoning for joining the Army when I heard that Reed had.

I'd needed to get away from all the ghosts that were haunting me.

The reason Reed's sister was dead was because of Jay. But, if I were being honest, I should've told someone with authority what was going on. What had happened to me.

My mom hadn't been enough. I should've gone to the police. Someone. Anyone.

My mother and Jay...they had a relationship that was like none I'd ever seen. The type where I knew, without any shadow of a doubt, that she would protect Jay. She'd side with him, regardless of whether or not what he was doing was wrong, because she believed her son could do no wrong.

When my mother had learned what Jay had done to me, she'd laughed in my face.

Laughed. In. My. Face.

She thought I was trying to get him in trouble because I had to clean up the bathroom when it wasn't my day.

She'd blamed me. Said I should stop playing around.

And when I explained to her that I wasn't joking or kidding at all—who the hell joked about their brother touching them inappropriately—she'd taken away my allowance. Told me that I didn't deserve it.

But, shortly after his freshman year had begun, something changed. Something happened that made him angry all the time. And something that caused a switch to flip inside of him, turning him into someone I didn't recognize.

It wouldn't be until I was in high school with him that I'd see what was going on at school. How he was bullied, ridiculed and treated like a pariah.

But, at that point, he'd been coming into my room at every night for a long time. I no longer cared what happened to him.

All the love that I'd once had for my brother had died.

All of my friends had disappeared, too. At least all of them but two. The ones that had stuck with me even when I'd tried my best to push everyone away.

I didn't have the best attitude.

I wasn't an easy friend to have.

It literally took everything Hennessy had to hold onto me that year. But, that was likely due to the fact that she was having her own problems at home. Problems that meant she was just as standoffish as I was at times.

Laryn had been trying to get me to spend time with her for a while, and the day that I'd finally relented, I met Reed.

Reed didn't know it, but he'd changed my life. He'd been the person who stopped me from withdrawing further into my shell. A shell I'd erected around me to keep all the pain at bay.

It also helped that my brother had started spending more time with Reed's brother, Tobias.

And, in turn, Reed's sister, Amy. He hadn't been inappropriate with Amy for their entire friendship. Lusting after her hadn't been enough and he started sneaking into her bed during the sleepovers.

If I had once suspected what was he was doing to Amy, I would've spoken up. I would've said something. Gone to the police. The grocery store manager that always asked me how I was doing. Hell, even the freaking shoe shop girl who looked at me like she could see through me. Like she knew something was wrong behind my fake smiles and even faker words.

Because had I known that Jay was doing some of the same things to Amy that he'd been doing to me, I wouldn't have stayed silent. I wouldn't have acted like everything was normal. I'd have said something.

Because I was like Amy. I'd experienced that for myself. Felt the horror of it and had thought, before I met Reed, about taking my life just like Amy had. That maybe it'd be easier to just stop living.

I'd been fourteen when Tobias and Jay had become best friends.

He'd changed everything, and again, he didn't even know it. Jay had started looking at Amy and stopped coming into my room.

What would he do if he had known? Would Amy still be alive? Would Jay?

Shuddering at the possibility of Jay still being here, and even possibly my parents, I got up and went in search of my dog.

I found him in the kitchen, staring longingly at the front door which Reed had disappeared through only hours before.

"Seriously?" I asked

Pepe Le Pew, or Pepe as he was better known, glanced at me over his shoulder, unimpressed.

"I don't know why you like him so much," I told him. "Seriously, you're my dog. Mine. He doesn't bathe you or bring you puppy cookies every day of your life."

He didn't answer me, he just turned his head back toward the door.

"Shit," I muttered under my breath. "Let's go."

The dog was definitely keeping me moving, even if I wanted nothing more than to lie on the couch and veg out while watching the newest season of *Game of Thrones*.

It was like he was keeping me from becoming a complete couch potato, thankfully.

When Pepe first saw Reed…it was rather heartbreaking. Almost like a child seeing his father for the first time after a long deployment.

Pepe had been ecstatic, and I think he might have actually fainted for a few seconds.

I hadn't realized that dogs fainted, but I'm pretty sure mine sure did the moment he saw Reed.

So yeah, that was heartbreaking to say the least.

It was as if Reed hadn't been gone for most of his life. It was as if they were best friends, all freakin' over again.

Shaking my head at the prospect of Pepe loving Reed more than me, I went to my bedroom, slipped on a pair of shorts—also Reed's that I'd taken back from Hennessy once I'd realized that my shorts were no longer a possibility—and found an old pair of tennis shoes.

Once I was dressed, I grabbed my purse, left my phone, and gestured to Pepe. "Let's go!"

He didn't need convincing.

We arrived at the new place fifteen minutes later, leaving me with an excitement that I hadn't felt since Reed had left.

This place...this place was—had always been—one of my favorite places in the world to go.

"Where do you want to go this time?" I asked my little dog.

He was looking this way and that, before deciding to take a path that led to the right and then back behind the house.

"Pepe, wait," I called to him.

He did, sitting down on his furry little hiney as he waited for me to get my shit together.

I swallowed, once again assaulted with the memories of this place.

It'd always been run down and abandoned.

But now that it was mine? Yeah, I couldn't wait to make it what Reed and I had always talked about—a happy place for our non-existent children at the time. It was going to be our home. It was going to be everything we'd ever imagined it would be.

It may be mine without Reed now, but at least I knew that it had once been a dream of both of ours.

Sighing, I started winding my way through the tall grass, following sedately behind Pepe, letting him explore while I looked at the world around me.

We'd gone about a half a mile when a weird *chink* sounded, like metal on metal, followed shortly by Pepe's high-pitched yelp.

And once again, my life tilted on its axis.

***

Hands stinging, I rushed into the veterinarian and, tears streaming down my face, cried out in panic.

"Dr. Castleberry!"

My eyes scanned the room the minute I rushed inside, and I saw him the moment my eyes swept over the front area where my friend, Lark, was sitting filling out some sort of paperwork.

I immediately rushed forward.

Dr. Castleberry abruptly turned into business mode, walking forward and bypassing everyone in the waiting room for me.

I held my heart out and hoped he was able to save him.

"What happened?" the old doc asked.

I went to wipe my eyes, but stopped when I saw the blood on my hands.

"The land I just bought has a bunch of old game traps on the property. On our walk today, Pepe stepped on one." I moaned, feeling like something was lodged deeply in the back of my throat. "I had to use a stick to get him out, but he struggled."

My stomach dropped, remembering again how my poor baby had struggled.

"Got it." The old doc barked, "Marissa. OR one. Now."

With that the two left, taking my deathly still puppy with them.

That's when I noticed that Lark was coming closer, gesturing me forward with her hands.

Lark cleaned up my arms and shirt as best as she could, but it was a futile effort. Something more than a simple wiping needed to be done—like throwing the shirt away completely. There was no way that all of this blood was coming out of the shirt. My favorite shirt of all time. The one and only shirt that I'd kept.

Goddammit.

I was starting to hyperventilate.

"Come back here and let's get your hands washed up." Lark snapped her fingers at me, making me blink in surprise.

I swallowed and nodded, my eyes going to the bloody paper towels in Lark's hand.

"Okay."

"Tell me about Pepe," she said, trying to get my mind out of my own personal hell.

"Pepe. Pepe Le Pew." I sniffled and walked to the large basin she'd indicated and washed my hands, ignoring the pain in them. "I got him when I was sixteen. Actually, Reed and I...err...I adopted him from the animal shelter. He was the cutest little thing. He's gone everywhere with me. Seen the world with me. He's my constant companion." I looked down at the blood swirling down the drain. "I can't do it without him."

"Do you want me to call Hennessy?"

Though I'd heard the words, I couldn't reply. My heart was shattering in a million tiny pieces.

"I'm all alone," I whispered painfully.

She touched my arm. "I'll go check on him. Bring you an update, okay?"

I nodded.

But I knew it was a useless effort on her part.

Pepe was gone.

Maybe not yet, but it wouldn't be long.

He'd lost a lot of blood. Too much blood.

And his poor body.

Had he been a bigger dog, the trap would've only taken his leg.

But this trap had been big, and my Pepe had been small.

So, so small.

Too small.

My little guy had always been small.

His size had been why I'd picked him at the shelter that day, all of those years ago.

***

12 ½ years ago

"You think my dad will let me keep him?" I whispered, looking down at the tiny puppy in my arms.

Reed shrugged. "Honestly? If he doesn't let you keep him, then we'll just take him to my apartment. I have a pet clause, but it's one hundred and fifty bucks."

I nodded, feeling a little giddy.

But later, as my mother stood there, looking at the dog, I realized my mistake.

She found something that I wanted and that meant that she could control me easier.

The fight that I'd had with my mother had been epic, but I got to keep the dog. Although, there were rules. One, I had to pay for the dog food. Two, I couldn't allow him to bark. Three, if he started to tear the house up, then he'd be gone.

Little did my mother know that Pepe would end up being the absolute perfect dog, and the only thing that stayed with me when I needed someone the most.

CHAPTER 13

Don't take advice from me. You'll just end up fucking drunk.
-Reed's secret thoughts

Reed

I was mid-exam, my fingers in a woman's unmentionables as I was checking her cervix for dilation, when a polite knock sounded at the door.

I ignored it, pulled my fingers out, and stripped off my glove.

"You're at a solid two dilated, but that's fairly normal at thirty-nine weeks. If you experience any more contractions, I want you to time them. If they get to three minutes apart or less, that's when it's time to go to the hospital. Okay?"

I offered her my hand and helped her to sitting, and she looked like she was ready to start freaking out all over again.

The first-time mother nodded her head, but her eyes went to her husband.

"Bags packed?" I asked.

He nodded, looking just as nervous as the mother.

I kept my laugh in check.

If he was freaked out now, I couldn't wait to see him during delivery.

"Alrighty, then." I threw my gloves into the trash and walked to the sink, washing my hands thoroughly.

Once I was through, I said my goodbyes, and paused when I saw the woman on the other side of the door.

Caria.

She just wouldn't catch the hint.

Every single time she made a move, I made sure to put myself well out of her reach, yet she just kept trying.

In all honestly, it was fucking annoying.

It was getting to the point where I wanted to report it to Torres.

"Yes?" I asked curtly.

Caria batted her eyelashes at me. "You have a patient in room four with what she suspects is an ectopic pregnancy."

I didn't want to reply to her, but for the sake of being a professional, I did anyway.

"Whose patient is she?"

"Dr. Torres," she answered.

"Is Dr. Torres busy?"

I could hear him fucking laughing about something in the breakroom, so he wasn't busy enough for Caria to be bringing his patient to me.

"Umm," she paused, trying to come up with something she could say to get her out of the mess I had a feeling she knew she'd gotten herself into.

Before I could tell her to go tell Dr. Torres about his patient, the door separating the inner office from the outer office slammed open, and my brother hurried inside.

"Baylor?"

"Lark called me," he said. "I tried to call you, but you're not fu-freakin' answering." He glanced around the office. "Krisney's dog was killed."

My stomach dropped.

"Caria, tell Torres I'm leaving."

***

When I arrived at the vet, Krisney wasn't there.

Lark was, though, and she looked extremely sad.

"What happened?" I asked, hurrying up to the counter.

She looked at me sadly. "The dog's leg was caught in a trap outside Krisney's property. He bled quite a bit and before we could repair the damage, he was already gone. But Reed, the problem is that kind of a wound shouldn't have caused that kind of blood loss. So Dr. Castleberry looked around in the chest cavity after he'd passed and found that he had cancer. All over. It was so bad, that the dog literally would've only had a few more weeks at most to live."

I felt like somebody had walked up to me and punched me directly in the chest.

"Does she know?"

Lark nodded. "We told her about an hour ago. She left with his body."

I didn't wait to reply to that.

I knew what she was going to do.

She was going to bury him, and I couldn't let her do that alone.

I didn't bother driving to her parents' place.

There was no way in hell that she was going to bury him there. Her parents had hated that dog, and honestly, Pepe hadn't been too fond of living there since he was forced to be in her room the entire time.

He was much happier once Krisney had moved out.

I drove to the old house, the memories assaulting me as I made my way to the place that used to be our refuge.

The old house was located directly next to the apartments that I used to reside in during my undergraduate studies.

The start of forty acres butted up right to the back door where my apartment had let out, and I let myself feel the excitement that always assaulted me when I pulled into the old driveway that looked like it needed updating way before even we came along.

I wasn't surprised to find Krisney's old car.

Nor was I surprised when I walked around the backside of the house to find her digging with a shovel.

Though, it did make me angry.

She wasn't overly pregnant yet, but she was still pregnant enough that she shouldn't be digging a fucking grave for a dog when she had a perfectly capable man to do the job for her.

"Kris," I called out, reaching for the shovel. "Let me do that."

She startled, and when I caught my first good look at her face, the nausea was back.

She was crying silent tears as she dug.

Fuck.

I dropped the shovel and pulled her into my chest, dropping my head to rest against her hair.

"I'm so sorry," I whispered.

I wish I'd have been here.

She sniffled against me, and I wrapped her tighter.

"He warned me," she swiped away tears.

I pulled back so only my arms were around her.

She stepped away even further, feeling like she was taking my heart straight out of my chest as she did.

"Who warned you?" I questioned, wanting to go to her so badly it hurt.

"The owner that I bought the property from. He said that there were some old traps out there, but I didn't give it thought, you know?"

I tilted my head, but didn't speak as I let her get out whatever she was trying to say.

And she didn't hesitate to continue.

"He said he wasn't in the right frame of mind when he came home from the war, and put up a lot of traps. But Reed, you and I were all over that land when we were younger. Never once did we see any traps."

We hadn't.

Though, we hadn't been warned about them, either.

"I should've taken his words to heart, but I didn't. I thought that since we'd been all over the land, that there weren't actually any out there. He said he'd done his best to clean them all up. If I'd known..."

"You didn't," I whispered. "You didn't know that there were any more out there. And honey, the doc told me that Pepe was sick anyway. He said he bled out too fast, from a small wound. They decided to have a look around while they had him opened up. He was riddled with cancer."

She shrugged.

So she knew.

"Baby," I brushed her hair out of her eyes. "You would've lost him anyway."

She swallowed, causing her throat to bob.

"Yeah, but I would've gotten extra time. I would've gotten to say goodbye."

With nothing else to say to that, I held her in my arms for as long as she would let me. When she finally pushed away, I got to digging.

When the hole was deep enough, I reached for the cloth-covered body that used to be Pepe, and lowered him into the ground.

At one point, I caught Krisney's movement out of the corner of my eye, and looked up to find her squatted down, her hands covering her face.

I felt sick to my stomach, watching this woman—my woman—go through something so terrible.

Not to mention she'd had to witness it in the first place.

But with dirt on my hands, and sweat pouring off of me, I stayed where I was and finished doing what I would never want Kris to have to do.

The moment that the last shovel full of dirt went onto the mound, I wiped my hands off on my scrub top and turned to find her still in the exact same position.

"Baby…"

My phone went off, and I sighed as I looked at the message.

"I have to go. It's a woman in labor." I apologized.

I went in to hug her to me once more, but she stopped me with an upraised hand.

"I don't think this is a good idea anymore." she whispered. "I want you to leave me alone, and when I come to your office, I want to see someone else."

I felt what felt like a lead balloon fall in my stomach.

"Kris…"

"Just go."

CHAPTER 14

I regret nothing.
-Krisney after she eats an entire family size box of Lucky Charms

Krisney

Avoiding him was incredibly hard when all I wanted to do was go to him.

The first time I felt the babies kick, I'd picked my phone up to call him, to tell him he needed to come over immediately. But then remembered that I needed to move on with my life and calling him to tell him wasn't a good idea. It was just letting the door swing back open when I'd tried with all my might to close it.

When I'd wake up in the middle of the night, my heart pounding a million miles an hour from a nightmare, I'd wanted nothing more than to call him and tell him about my dreams.

I never did.

Then, when I'd see everyone in town and take in their judgment—I wished for nothing more than to have him at my side.

He'd tried to be there.

After the day Pepe died, he'd tried relentlessly to insert himself back in my life, but I'd done everything in my power to make sure that that didn't happen.

The only thing I wasn't able to accomplish was getting a new doctor.

Torres and the other doctor practicing with Reed in the office wouldn't take me as a patient.

I'd heard through the grapevine that Reed had told them in no uncertain terms that if they took me on, he'd leave.

And since the practice was so swamped, they'd refused to take me on.

Meaning that three months after telling him that I wanted nothing to do with him, I still had to see him at least once a month.

This would be my third month seeing him, and I'd been shoring up my defenses ever since the last appointment.

***

"They're moving well?" he asked excitedly.

I nodded, unwilling to speak unless I absolutely had to.

I didn't want to chance telling him that I loved him, I missed him, and I wanted him to move in with me so I didn't have to have his babies alone.

Hence the staying quiet bit.

My emotions were fucking everywhere, and I knew that if I could just get through this appointment, that I would make it another day without him.

I would.

He started to massage my stomach, and I had to clench my legs together to keep from jolting at the contact.

I knew this wasn't anything sexual in nature in the least, but all he had to do was touch me, and I was panting for him.

I gritted my teeth when he moved down to just above my pubic bone.

"You feel this?"

172

My hand automatically went to his, and he guided my hand and pushed. I felt something round and hard.

"Yes," I croaked.

"That's a butt." He laughed. "And this up here…" He moved my hand to a spot just above that. "That's the head of baby A."

The head was sideways by my lower ribs on my left side.

"This is baby B, head here." He moved my hand again to my upper ribs, then pressed. "And this is the back."

"How do you know this?" I blurted as he moved my hand down the length of the baby's back.

"Practice," he said, his eyes meeting mine.

They were happy.

He was happy.

And if I was being honest, I was the happiest I'd been since the last appointment.

"I start a new job on Monday," I told him.

He held my eyes.

"Where?"

"At the dentist on Main Street. His old dental hygienist quit."

Reed's laugh was happy.

"That's good news. I wasn't sure you were going to get to utilize your degree."

I'd gotten my degree in dental hygiene while in the Army and then had practiced somewhat in Alabama when I was in the Reserves. When I was sent to Germany, it'd been for my old job—which was a whole bunch of office work that I realized rather quickly that I was no longer cut out for.

That'd been the deciding factor to wait until I found a job that I knew I'd stay at, and not do one just for the temporary while I looked for a new one. That wasn't fair to the employer or to me.

"I'm thinking it's good news, too. He also said that maternity leave won't be a problem, because the old dental hygienist is willing to come back while I'm out for the six weeks."

He nodded, giving my stomach one last press, before he pulled away.

"You know what today is?"

I nodded.

That'd been another reason why I was anxious.

It was the exam that would tell me what the sex of the babies I was carrying were.

After one more lingering glance at my belly, he stood up and walked to the sink where he washed his hands out of habit.

I tried not to be offended that he would think he'd need to wash his hands, and struggled to get up.

I was forty seven months pregnant with twins, and I felt like I was as big as a house.

I probably looked it, too.

Yet, the scale at the front of the office told me that I'd only gained my original twenty pounds.

Which was surprising since I was eating everything in sight.

Neither the nurse nor Reed seemed to be worried, though, so I chose to count that as a good thing as I tried not to think about my eating habits.

I'd just barely made it up onto my elbows when Reed was there, helping me to sit.

"Sorry," he muttered, immediately releasing me once he had me in an upright position.

I bit my lip to keep from crying out at the loss, and made my way up to standing.

Once he was sure I was steady, he walked to the door and opened it, allowing me to exit in front of him.

I did, and I tried not to think about the way I was walking away from him yet again.

I hated leaving.

The only time I ever felt happy was when I was with him.

Pregnancy fucking sucked, because all I ever thought about was him...my babies that I got pregnant with by him. What he was doing. Where he was at. Whose baby he was delivering.

It just kept getting worse and worse, and I wasn't sure how much longer I could handle staying away.

I might just beg him for anything, admitting that I was an utter moron for telling him to stay away.

Scraps were better than nothing—that I was quickly realizing.

"Caria, please let everyone know that I'm headed to the ultrasound with my...Kris." He gestured to me with his head.

Caria's eyes flashed, then she nodded.

Reed, however, didn't notice. His eyes were all for me as he gestured to the door. "Let's go."

He was practically bouncing in his pretty, bright yellow shoes.

I wanted them. I was so transfixed on them that I didn't think to even ask why he was going with me. I knew where the ultrasound floor was. I also had taken the path quite a few times before, mostly because also on the same floor was the lab that I had to do my sugar testing at the week prior.

"Krisney?"

I looked up, startled to find Reed that close, and blinked. "Yes?"

"What are you looking at?"

"Your shoes," I told him. "They're pretty."

His mouth kicked up into a grin. "I like them, too."

I didn't say anything to that.

I couldn't.

His smile was enough to make me feel like I'd been kicked in the stomach.

Absently I rubbed my hand over my belly, smiling slightly when a foot kicked out at where my hand was resting.

"Are they moving again?"

He pressed the button for the elevator, looking at me, waiting for me to answer.

"Yes," I said, stepping onto the elevator once the doors opened. "You can feel."

His eyes took in my sincerity, and then he reached forward, almost hesitantly, and put his hands back onto my belly.

This time it was different.

This time, there wasn't anything he was doing that I could blame on him being a doctor.

No, this time, it was out of pure pleasure.

And I could read that pleasure all over his face.

Moments after his hand met my stomach, I felt a rather rambunctious kick slam right into his palm.

And the smile that he awarded me with was nothing less than euphoric.

"I wonder what they are…"

The doors slid open, and he stepped away.

Immediately I missed his heat.

I was also mad at inanimate objects—IE the elevator doors—for opening when all I wanted him to do was never stop touching me. Not ever again.

Goddammit, I was such a loser.

I was the one who told him to stay away.

I was the one who…

"You coming?"

I shook off my temporary insanity and hurried behind him, trying in vain to keep up with his long strides.

"Slow down, Daddy Long Legs," I called, hurrying after him.

There was only so much I could do, though, seeing as I had such short legs.

"Sorry, Caterpillar."

I snorted, remembering how we'd come up with those stupid nicknames all those years ago.

In fact, it'd been something similar to what had just happened, and he'd called me that because I was a slow, short-legged person. I'd called him daddy long legs because he was so fast.

The bad part? He didn't even blink when he called me that. It was as if he'd called me that numerous times, as if the last time he'd said that had only been just yesterday, instead of a lifetime ago.

Fucking hell.

Then, he had to go and make matters worse by grabbing my hand, leading me through the office, and straight back to the ultrasound room, bypassing not just the waiting room, but the ultrasound room I'd used the last time I was there.

"Uhhh," I started to say, but was interrupted when a happy-go-lucky voice filled the hallways, seeming to bounce off the walls. "Reed, my boy!"

I laughed when I saw a man, much older than Reed, walking down the hall toward us.

He may be old, but there was no way in hell the man was out of shape.

He had to run or something, because Jesus Christ he was tall and fit.

"Hey, Boyce. We're here to get the Hail babies checked out and over."

The man looked at me, and his eyes changed.

"I had no clue that it was that Hail."

Reed laughed, and I felt like I was left out in the dark on who this man was to Reed. I'd never seen him in my life, and honestly, I knew everyone here.

This man, though?

Never seen him before.

"I'm glad you could follow me back here. I was worried about you."

Reed's words had me glancing back between the two men like an annoying bobble head doll.

"Oh, shoot," Reed said. "Boyce, this is Krisney. Krisney, this is Boyce, he's a...used to be a sonographer with the Army. He's retired now, and he moved back here, what was it...a month ago?"

Reed turned to Boyce, and Boyce nodded his head. "It was time. It's nice to meet you, Krisney."

I smiled.

"Boyce is gonna do all the fun stuff today."

My brows rose at that.

Reed winked at me, though, understanding my hesitation. "It'll be okay."

With that, he led us into a second room, and this time it was with a huge fucking couch off to one corner of the room. The exam table was smack dab in the middle of it, and the biggest TV I'd ever seen was taking up the wall across from the couch and the table.

Reed didn't take the couch, though.

He took my hand and helped me up onto the table, and then stood beside me while shoving up my shirt.

I would've laughed if I hadn't liked seeing him so excited.

"Do y'all want to know the sex of the baby?"

"Babies," Reed corrected, then looked down at me. "Do we want to know?"

I'd originally planned on saying yes. But what came out was a resounding, "No!"

Reed looked like I'd ran over his pet cat. "Really?"

"Really," I confirmed.

He sighed. "I guess that was what we'd planned on doing from the very beginning, anyway. I just never expected you to actually go through with it."

When he said from the 'very beginning' he really meant the very, very beginning. We'd talked about children on our second date.

I'd told him that I didn't want to know. That I wanted to be surprised. To find out the sex of our babies with him in the delivery room.

Oh, if I only I knew how wrong I'd be.

If I'd known, I would've found out right then and there.

***

"Any problems you want Dr. Hail to be aware of?"

I shook my head.

"Good."

I paused, remembering something.

"These stretch marks, though," I muttered, lifting my shirt slightly and showing Reed's nurse.

The nurse grimaced right along with me.

"Those are going to be there forever."

That came from the bitch that hated my guts.

I had a feeling that she and Reed had something going on before I came along and 'ruined things' by showing up pregnant.

Then again, at this point, they could have started something right back up.

I'd left Reed standing only a foot away from Pepe's grave over three months ago, and I had stuck with my guns ever since.

After our last doctor appointment, I'd left him standing in the elevator, watching me leave with a sad expression on his face.

But I couldn't help it.

I needed to protect me at this point, not Reed.

And that was what I'd planned on doing.

But Caria? Yeah, I fucking hated her. With a passion.

I was blaming it on the hormones, but I knew had I not been pregnant, I still would've hated her just as much.

I'd seen her around town before with him. Once last week while at Subway, and another time while at the gas station when I'd been filling up. They'd been getting coffee.

I never got the confirmation, but I tried valiantly not to think about what Reed might or might not have done with her.

It hurt too bad.

Literally, every time I even came close to thinking about it, I was reminded that though we now shared children together that would be born in a few months, we weren't anything more than that.

We were still in the same exact spot as we'd been when this all started.

Apart.

"I've heard using the stretch mark lotion doesn't really help," Reed's nurse, Opal, interrupted my inner musings. "You're just spending the extra money on it when you could get the same results from using the Wal-Mart brand."

I grimaced.

That'd been what I'd been using.

Shit.

"Well, what the heck do I use now?" I muttered almost to myself.

Opal patted my hand as she finished up with my blood pressure, and I stood up while also stretching my back.

Who knew having two kids growing inside of you would cause a relatively healthy woman to feel this much pain?

There wasn't a day that went by that I didn't have something that hurt. And the more days that passed, the more stuff that hurt.

Yesterday it was my feet. Today, it was my feet and pubic bone. Next week, it'd be my entire body, I just knew it.

"You should try this." Reed's whatever the hell she was, ex hopefully, lifted a clear bottle and wiggled it at me.

I looked at the bottle and frowned.

"Oh, it's okay. Caria sells essential oil," Opal said, reading the hesitancy on my face. "She's the oil guru around here. Just last week she gave some to Reed to help him sleep. Lavender, was it?"

I wanted to throat punch this 'Caria' chick. I'd never heard her name before, or even heard her mentioned around town, but maybe there was a reason for that.

Maybe they were trying to protect me.

Maybe, Reed really did have feelings for this chick.

"What's in it?"

"It's Patchouli oil. Patchouli helps recovery of the skin, and prevents ugly scarring, like what you've got going on there," Caria explained, holding the simple bottle out.

I took it, mostly because Opal was staring at me as if to say, 'Well?'

"What do I do with it? Just rub it on?" I asked. "And is it safe during pregnancy?"

Caria nodded, her face impassive, and said, "Yes. Completely, one hundred percent safe."

Opal started to nod right along with Caria, and if it hadn't been for Opal's agreement, I might've thought that this oil she was giving me was poisoned.

But as I looked at the bottle, I realized that it was actually pretty damn official looking.

"You sell this oil?"

Caria nodded. "On my website."

She then proceeded to pull out a card and handed it to me.

I took it, looking at the words on the little rectangle, and then nodded my head. "Thank you."

"Kris..." Reed said, surprising the three of us.

Opal grinned. "I'll see you in a moment, dearie. I need to go give a call to an insurance agency."

With that Opal left, leaving only Caria—who was staring at Reed with such uninhibited devotion in her eyes—and me.

"Hey," I said, clearing my voice. "How are you?"

Caria moved until she was standing next to Reed's side.

"How are you?"

"She's good. She said something about stretch marks, though. I gave her some oil to help with them."

Reed didn't even glance at her.

"Caria," Reed said. "Would you mind leaving? I'd like to spend a few minutes alone with Krisney."

I wanted to whoop in excitement that he'd told her to leave.

In fact, if I could rub her nose in it, I would.

"Do you want to go to lunch?"

Reed's question startled me.

I wanted nothing more than to spend more time with him, but I couldn't do it. I'd been doing so well.

He took in my hesitation, and likely my decision to say no. "I want to talk…I want to figure some things out."

I wanted that, too.

This not talking about the obvious thing we were doing was starting to grate on my nerves.

"Okay," I whispered.

He nodded, looking thankful.

"I know that the PA saw you, but do you have any questions?"

The PA for the office was having to work in three doctors' patients today because all three of the doctors had been out of the office delivering babies.

I hadn't expected Reed to be back.

Which had been what gave me a false sense of hope.

I'd let my guard down, thinking he wasn't here.

Now I had to go to lunch with him.

Shit.

He winked at me and offered me his outstretched forearm.

"Let's go."

I took it, unsure whether this was a good idea or not.

He led me out of the room, down the hall, and to the door that separated the waiting room from the main office.

"Oh, hold on." He held up a finger. "I bought you something."

Then he was gone, leaving me standing there all alone.

I pushed the door open, thinking I'd wait in the hallway for him, when my name was called.

I turned and saw Opal heading toward me, stopping me before I could reach the door.

"Hey!"

I smiled when I saw her.

"Yes?"

"Caria said this tea would help with indigestion and is supposed to help with sleep. You were saying how it's affecting you badly in the evenings. This'll help with that. I take it myself sometimes." Opal handed me the box.

I took it, again thinking that Caria had some ulterior motive in giving me things.

I took the box, knowing that I would likely not drink it.

But I hadn't counted on Reed's bombshell he'd dropped on me moments after walking into the Taco Shop, either.

CHAPTER 15

I really do try to see the best in people. But with morning people,
sometimes it's too damn hard.
-Krisney's secret thoughts

Krisney

I woke up with the worst pain I'd ever experienced.

My stomach felt like somebody had kicked it, and I immediately knew that something was very wrong.

I sat up, disoriented, and stared at the wall.

All I could think about was the words Reed had uttered to me over lunch.

I want a chance.

I moaned when another wave of agony rolled through me.

Then I felt something wet between my legs, and it definitely wasn't from my dreams of Reed.

No, there was just way too much for it ever to be considered that.

I reached for my phone, and dialed Reed.

***

Reed

"Did you use anything, or take anything?" Dr. Torres asked. "Did you take anything new that you've never had before?"

The pain was etched all over Krisney's face.

"The only thing new that I've done over the last twenty-four hours is the essential oil that was given to me by a nurse at your office, Caria. She gave me some Patchouli oil for my stretch marks."

Dr. Torres wrote it down, then went to his phone to look up the side effects of that oil.

I ran my rough hand down the soft skin of Krisney's arm, but she didn't look at me.

"What about that tea?" I paused, remembering something she'd taken. "Did you drink that?"

Krisney's face fell, and her eyes finally met mine. "Yes."

"Do you remember what it was?"

"She said chamomile. It was in the box still. That's at home, though." She shook her head as another pain rocked her, and I looked to the monitor to see that another contraction had hit.

I looked in frustration at the other medicine that wasn't doing a damn thing to stop her labor from progressing, and instantly felt a wave of disappointment roll through me.

If we couldn't get her contractions to stop, we wouldn't have a choice but to deliver the babies today.

Eight weeks early.

A lifetime when it came to a preemie baby.

"Nothing else?" Dr. Torres asked, sounding worried himself.

When the drugs wouldn't work the way that they were supposed to, we'd tried alternate means. When those hadn't worked, we'd started questioning *why*.

Which led us to this point.

"Nothing but the oil that Caria gave me." Krisney moaned.

"What kind of oil was it again?" I asked her as I pulled out my phone.

She closed her eyes, and a tear slipped free.

"Patchouli?" She shrugged, gesturing to the bag I'd grabbed for her on my way out her door with her in my arms only two hours before. "I think. I'm not sure the exact name. It's in my purse, though."

I walked forward and took the bottle out of her purse. It was the same bottle type as the one that Caria had given me lavender oil in last week. Why she'd given me the lavender oil, I didn't know. But she had. Being a generally nice person, I took it. It was still sitting on the desk in my office at work.

I wasn't sure what I was supposed to do with it, but I'd taken it because I tried not to look like the complete dick that I was in my place of work.

Palming the bottle in my hand, I handed it over to the nurse who was closest to me.

"Take this down to the lab, and see what the hell is in it." I paused. "And tell them this is a rush. To do it in the next ten minutes, or I'm coming down there myself to do it."

The nurse nodded her head and rushed out of the room.

Dr. Torres and I weren't the only ones worried.

I didn't think it would be anything bad. Not really. I was just being thorough.

We couldn't get the contractions to stop, and there had to be a reason why.

That was just the most obvious reason at this point.

And, when the call came nine minutes later as to what was in the bottle, I grew confused.

"It's Pennyroyal," the lab tech said the moment I answered. "Do you know what that is?"

"I'll look it up," I said, then hung up before the lab tech could tell me what it was.

Pennyroyal.

Pennyroyal.

Why did that sound so familiar?

I pulled out my phone and did a quick search, and my heart fell.

"Pennyroyal. Side effects for pregnant and breastfeeding: If you are pregnant or breastfeeding, it is LIKELY UNSAFE to take pennyroyal by mouth or apply it to your skin. There is some evidence that pennyroyal oil can cause abortions by causing the uterus to contract. But the dose needed for this effect could kill the mother or cause her life-long kidney and liver damage. Pennyroyal leaf tea seems to be able to start menstruation, which could also threaten a pregnancy," I read aloud.

The doctor with me, Torres, swore so loudly that a nurse came in from outside.

"She was given that, wasn't she?"

I looked over to see tears in Krisney's eyes.

"I didn't know. I swear, I didn't know." She started to weep, and I wanted nothing more than to bring her in my arms and tell her that it would be okay. But I knew it wouldn't be okay.

Whatever she'd ingested, both orally and transdermally, had been enough to induce labor.

Seeing as she was thirty-two weeks, the babies, if born today, would have a long road ahead of them. And, since they were twins, they were already smaller than normal thirty-two weekers.

"It also says that the side effects of the pennyroyal could cause liver, kidney, and sometimes nervous system damage," I told Torres.

"That would account for the odd kidney function test," Torres said. "We attributed it to the pregnancy, but it's more than likely due to the oil. I think it's best to get the babies out, so that whatever affects it had on Krisney, the babies don't have to have, too."

I agreed.

When my eyes met Krisney's, I saw resignation there.

Sorrow, regret and disgust followed soon after.

"It'll be okay," I told her. "We'll get through this."

Krisney looked away.

"Just get them out. Make sure they're safe."

***

The babies were born by Caesarian section two hours later.

Two hours after that, Krisney was in the first stages of both liver and kidney failure.

CHAPTER 16

Life sucks then you die.
-T-shirt

Reed

"The damage is too severe," the physician, Dr. Albert Morris, that had taken over Krisney's case said. "Her liver function, as well as kidney function, are at less than fifteen percent at this point. It's been less than eight hours. I expect, by this time tomorrow, all function will be non-existent."

"So, what does that mean?" I asked.

I knew the basics, of course.

I'd become an MD, after all.

But I was hoping, despite knowing, that he'd have an alternative that I hadn't thought of yet.

"She needs a new kidney, and a new liver," he told me bluntly. "There is no other option for her at this point. With one, or the other, we could've worked with it. With both, as well as her weakness from the birth…well, her prognosis is not good."

With that heartbreaking, final news, he patted me sharply on the shoulder and left the room, leaving me looking at the broken woman who had just had her life taken away from her.

***

I slammed through the last of the hospital doors and came face to face with my entire family.

They were all standing there, looking at me expectantly.

"She's dying."

"What?" That was Travis.

"Dying. They expect her liver and kidneys to fail by this time tomorrow, if not sooner," I told them, feeling numb.

"There's nothing they can do?" Dante asked.

I couldn't even scrounge up enough happiness to see Dante there. He'd been practically non-existent in our lives since his family had died…and now I knew how he felt.

I closed my eyes as tears threatened to take over.

"She can get a new kidney, as well as a new liver," I said. "But the donor registry won't accept her at this moment in time. She's too high risk. They have other, more healthy candidates that would have a much higher percentage of surviving at this point that they won't even consider her."

"Test us," my brother said.

I looked over at Baylor.

I closed my eyes and dropped my head.

"It's not that easy," I said. "There has to be an exact match. *Exact.*"

"How will you know unless you try?"

That came from Hannah, Travis's wife.

She was right.

"But y'all have kids," I said. "Young babies…"

"Test us."

That came from Evander.

I dropped my head even further into my hands. "I'm headed down there myself."

***

What felt like days later, but was likely only hours, the nurse walked in with a giant smile on her face.

"You're a perfect match," she said, handing over the papers.

I took the papers and scanned over them, making sure that they weren't fucking with me.

Not that I thought they would, but this was better than anything I could've ever hoped for.

"I'm a perfect match." I handed the page to Dr. Morris.

The doctor looked over my test on his own this time and nodded his head.

"Perfect," he agreed.

My eyes closed, as relief poured through me.

The last eight hours, as we all waited for the results of our tests, had been agonizing.

Each hour that passed, I watched Krisney deteriorate just a little bit more.

"Do it now."

"No!"

I looked over at my mother, not feeling a thing.

"Yes."

"No." She stood up. "I'm not losing another one of my children!"

The room went absolutely quiet.

Anger poured over me, though.

"You can't mean that."

My mother crossed her arms over her chest.

"I've had two of my children die, Reed Hail. I'm not allowing you to do this," she persisted. "You won't understand…"

I stood up.

"I won't understand?" I asked. "I have two children, right now, fighting for their lives. The woman I love, the woman I've loved since we were young, is now fighting for her life and likely won't make it until tomorrow without me. I'm doing this, whether you like it or not."

She turned her back on me. "Well, then I won't be here when you do it."

With that she left, leaving me to stare at her in disbelief that she said what she did.

"Thank fucking Christ you finally admitted it," Travis muttered. "It's about fucking time."

I looked over at my brother, surprised to see not just him, but my entire fucking family, standing there.

"What?" he asked.

That was when Baylor, my other brother, entered the conversation.

"Takes her almost dying for you to say something," Baylor muttered.

"Y'all…" Baylor's new woman, Lark, said. "This is not the time."

No, it wasn't.

I turned toward the doc. "Tell me what we need to do."

"Insurance…"

I waved that off. "I don't care. I don't care who gets billed for it. Yes, I have an emotional attachment to the patient. No, I don't care if it's going to be a problem. Just get it done."

"Get 'er dun!" Travis teased.

"Umm," the transplant specialist said to the family members in the room. "Would you mind waiting outside? We have some things to discuss."

I flipped Travis off discreetly as he left, no longer in the same state of mind that I'd been in earlier thanks to knowing that I wouldn't have to watch the love of my life die.

He started to laugh and went back outside, waiting for me to come out and let everyone know what was going on.

"Tell me what I need to know."

***

Krisney

"Don't do this."

My eyes fluttered open, and I struggled to keep them open as I looked around the room.

"Give me one good reason, Mom."

A flutter of happiness flitted through me.

That was Reed's voice. It didn't matter where I was, or what I was feeling. The man's voice always made me happy.

Always.

Sad, hungry. *Dying.*

It didn't matter. The man had a way about him.

"You could die," Reed's mother snapped.

Silence followed that proclamation.

"If I don't do this, she'll die." He paused. "I don't think I could survive her death, Mom," he growled in frustration. "I could die crossing the street on the way to get coffee in ten minutes. Tomorrow, I could not wake up, having passed away in my sleep. I know better than anyone that life isn't always promised. I have to do it. I have to save her, even if that means giving her everything I have to give."

Something terrible started to churn in my belly.

What were they talking about?

"A hepatectomy is a big deal, Reed. This isn't just a surgery that you get up and walk away from. And we aren't even mentioning the probability of a kidney transplant, also.

"Not to mention the potential bleeding problems you could suffer once you've gone through with the surgery," she continued. "And honestly, you have two children now. It's time to stop thinking with your heart and using your brain. They need you."

Children? What?

And then it all came back to me in one huge blow straight to my heart.

I'd gone into labor. But the labor hadn't been normal. Everything had been wrong. The doctors couldn't get my contractions to stop. My liver and kidneys were failing. And I'd had to deliver our babies eight weeks early.

Oh, and I was dying.

My head moved, and I found him.

Reed was sitting at the end of my bed, pouring through a chart. His eyes were scanning the pages like only a doctor would. A doctor that was trying desperately to save a patient. He was searching for something that he wasn't going to find.

"Mom..."

"You haven't even seen them!" *He hadn't?*

"You haven't gone to see them?"

Reed and his mother's heads snapped toward me.

Reed was on his feet moments later.

"I haven't."

"Why?"

"Because I don't want to see them without you. I want you with me when we see them for the first time. I don't want to experience that alone."

"Reed..."

"You're getting a new kidney, and part of a liver."

"Whose?"

If I remembered correctly, my prognosis wasn't good. And they wouldn't even put me on the donors list.

So, if I was getting a liver...it had to be from someone I knew.

Reed.

"Reed, no," I whispered. "You can't."

"It's not that I don't want you to live."

My eyes moved to his mother.

"What?"

"I have never blamed you."

Tears started to form in my eyes.

"I don't want him to do this, either." I swallowed. My voice sounded so weak, and it was scary.

"I love him more than life, but I would never be okay with this. And you're right. He has someone—two someones—to live for now."

She smiled at me sadly.

"You'll always come first to him." She looked down at her hands. "He'll do anything to make you happy. Even going to see his babies that he refused to see because he wanted to experience that with you."

I swallowed past the lump in my throat.

"I'm going to die."

Her eyes sliced to mine. "Then you'll take him with you."

I looked away. It was the hardest thing to do in my life.

"You never saw him like I saw him after he broke up with you. But he's never been the same since. He loves you. Has never stopped loving you." I heard the tears in her voice. "That day irrevocably changed so many lives. My daughter's. Your brother's. Yours. Reed's." She cleared her throat.

"Nobody more than yours and Reed's, though." She exhaled. "I'm happy and sad to have him back. And the reason I have him back is because you're dying. I don't know what to say. What to feel."

CHAPTER 17

Shut up and take my kidney.
-Reed under the influence of anesthesia

Reed

Day 1

"Is she done?"

I didn't ask it to anyone in particular. My brothers. One of them. I was fairly sure my mother wasn't there. So, no need to ask her.

"No."

"Did it go all right?"

"Yours or hers?"

Why the hell would I care about mine?

"Hers."

"Still in surgery, bro." I think it was Baylor who said it. "I'll wake you when it's done."

***

Day 2

"Is she okay?"

I couldn't find the strength to open my eyes. I couldn't lift my hand, either.

201

"She's fine," a feminine voice said. "She made it through surgery. Hennessy is sitting with her right now. She hasn't woken though."

Hannah, Travis's wife.

"When she wakes, let me know," I ordered.

"What about her kidney function?"

Hannah's laughter followed me into sleep.

***

Day 3

My eyes opened, and for the first time I felt like keeping them open.

I looked around the room and found it empty.

My heart lurched.

I pressed the call button at my bedside, heart hammering, and waited.

It didn't take long for a nurse to arrive.

The minute she saw me, awake and alert, she smiled.

"Your family said if you woke up and they still weren't here, that I was to tell you she made it through surgery.

"She's not awake yet, but she's showing signs when stimulated. And both kidney and liver seem to be functioning correctly. As for you, you've been in and out. I think this is the most awake I've seen you."

I didn't care about me. I cared about her. And my babies.

Fuck.

"What about the babies?" I found myself asking cautiously.

"Both are fighting. That's where everyone is. It's visiting hours."

My belly seemed to warm from the inside out.

"Good."

I was glad they weren't alone.

"Have they gained any weight?"

What had it been now? One? Two days?

"Two days since your surgery. Three days since they were born." I must've voiced that last question aloud. Huh. "And they've both lost a little bit of weight, but they're not concerned about it yet."

That fucking sucked.

"Can I go see Kris?" I asked, feeling much more awake now.

The nurse smiled. "The doctor said you were going to ask that. And yes, as long as you don't overdo it, we can do that."

"What happened with me?" I asked as I slowly made to sit up.

The nurse came to my side and waited, allowing me to make the moves without help, and I appreciated it.

"You had a reaction to the anesthesia," she answered, backing up when I finally swung my legs over the side of the bed. "They were a little worried at first due to your initial response but you seemed to rally well."

"My initial response?"

She looked at me funny.

"They discussed this yesterday with you." She paused. "Do you not remember?"

I shook my head, then took a deep breath and stood.

The pain was terrible.

In fact, on a scale of one to I've never felt this kind of pain before, I was at 'I'm going to cry.'

But I stood up anyway and walked—more like shuffled—the two steps with her standing in front of me, ready to catch me if I fell.

I didn't, thank fuck.

"Take a seat. I'll grab your cath bag and your IV stand."

I did, not thinking about my catheter, or anything else.

My anticipation of seeing Krisney was too strong, and overrode all my embarrassment at having to deal with the aftermath of a catheter.

"There we go," she handed the bag to me. "As for your initial response to anesthesia—it'll be in your chart from now on that you don't respond well to it. You nearly died."

I looked down, the doctor in me studying the color and amount of urine in the bag.

"Everything good with me now?"

"Urine output is perfect," she answered. "Liver function, so far so good."

I nodded, then hooked the bag on the arm rest and started to rearrange wires so we could move.

"I'm still in the ICU?"

She shook her head. "No. You're a floor below."

"Krisney?"

"Still in the ICU. If she keeps improving, and wakes up soon, though, they'll move her," she answered. I frowned at that, wondering how she knew all of this. "I just got off the phone with her doctor when you paged."

I nodded, understanding her answer.

"Take me."

She grinned.

"Two shakes," she said. "I have to…there we go."

She pushed the brakes off, and then swung me around, leading me at a fast pace out of my room and straight to the elevator.

I'd been in this wing before seeing a patient who'd had a stroke after she'd delivered, and it was completely different seeing it from a patient's perspective rather than a doctor's.

Two minutes later, but what felt like two hours, I was being pushed into a room that was similar to mine.

Only, this room had a glass wall that was so close to the nurses' station that we might as well have been standing in it.

"I'll leave you for a while," the nurse said. "Twenty minutes. That's it, okay?"

She likely shouldn't even be doing that, but I was appreciative of her taking care of me, and allowing me the time to see the woman that held a large portion of my heart.

The moment the glass door closed, I looked over at the deathly pale woman on the bed, and shivered.

"I'm so sorry."

I reached for her hand, but it didn't curl around mine.

I squeezed, but she didn't squeeze back.

***

Day 4

I took my own catheter out.

That was likely not what should've been done, and I'd hear about it later, but I wasn't in the mood to be tethered to it anymore.

I could measure my own urine output, thank you very much.

Once that was taken care of, I came out of the bathroom with just a single wire attached to me, and even that was coming out once I had the proper tools—IE a fucking Band-Aid—to take care of it.

Hannah was there, watching me, when I came out.

"You want some help?"

I offered her my hand.

I didn't know my brothers' wives all that well. With me living in Alabama when I was home, and being in the Army and then the Reserves, I hadn't had much time to get to know them all.

Hannah, though, was one of my favorites.

Then again, they all were, really, in their own way.

My eyes skidded to a stop when I saw Hennessy standing in the doorway.

"She's awake."

I didn't wait for the damn Band-Aid.

I shuffled out of my room, and down the hall, not giving one flying fuck that my ass was partially exposed, or that I was somewhat bleeding.

Hennessy stayed at my side.

"She's mad at you."

I grinned.

"Is she now?"

"Apparently, she figured out that you never went and saw the babies and is now demanding that you offer her compensation."

I would've laughed had I not been worried about how badly it would hurt.

"A kidney and a half a liver aren't enough?" I teased, pressing the button for the elevator.

The nurses I passed on their way to lunch just shook their heads, knowing that they couldn't control me.

I waved, pressed the button for the floor above ours, and waited for the doors to close.

"She's mad about that, too." She paused. "I think she's just mad in general at this point."

I couldn't keep the smile off my face. Not on the trip down the hallway. Not on the way into the room, and definitely not, when I saw Krisney's angry eyes staring back at me.

"You."

"Me." I smiled wider.

She narrowed her eyes. "You promised."

I shrugged. "I also made a promise to you a long time ago, too. I'd see them with you. I'm holding to your first promise you took from me."

I knew it was wrong.

But with my family rotating through visiting them, as well as my own mother working there, I knew they were getting visitors.

And, they were doing extremely well.

Had they not, I would've gone to see them.

But I'd already broken so many promises, and this was one I couldn't break. It just felt like, deep inside my heart, something I had to do.

"You're such an ass." She shook her head. "And I'm really, really not happy with you."

***

Day 5

"You're free to go, Mr. Hail," the nurse said as she handed me my papers. "I have a feeling I'll be seeing you again, though."

I just rolled my eyes.

Then I got out and walked next door to where Krisney was just getting settled.

"Honey, I'm home," I teased as I walked in.

Hennessy rolled her eyes.

"You're so weird."

CHAPTER 18

*Do you ever laugh at something that is really dark, and then
wonder what the hell is wrong with you?
-Text from Travis to Reed*

Krisney

"What are you doing here?"

Reed gave me a look that clearly said, without words, that he
thought I was crazy.

"I'm here to watch you recover," he said. "They're even bringing
my old bed in here. He paused, then grinned. "Here it is now."

The orderly rolled it in and put it in the corner of the room, waved
at Reed, and then left just as fast.

I narrowed my eyes.

"Henn," I said softly. "Do you think you could give me and Reed a
few minutes alone?"

Hennessy didn't bother to argue, just got up and left.

The moment the door closed softly behind her, I turned my
attention back to Reed.

"If you're going to break my heart, just break it."

I choked on the words, and his head snapped in my direction.

"What are you talking about?"

"I can't live like this." I blew out a breath to keep the tears at bay. "You're hurting my heart. I don't know if we're together. I don't know, from one day to the next, if you're going to be nice Reed or mean Reed. Or used to not, anyway. Now you're just all smiles and shit, and it's fucking with my head. Before…sometimes you say the nicest things, and then others you look at me like I'm the antichrist."

"I do not."

His words were adamant, but I couldn't help but shake my head. "You do…did."

He looked so confused that I almost stopped and reevaluated if this was the right time and place to do this, but I couldn't do this. It was seriously messing with my head to have him here.

My stupid heart was starting to feel that maybe he was there to stay…so if he wasn't, I needed to know.

"I was…I'm all in."

"You're all in."

"All in," he confirmed.

"What changed?" I asked, staring at him.

"Nearly losing you."

I laughed. "You could've lost me at any time. That's a stupid reason."

His eyes changed as he took a seat and stared at me across his bed.

"I can't ever make it up to you," he murmured gruffly. "I can only go on from here. I didn't want to hurt anybody. My mom was in pain. Hell, I was in pain. I couldn't believe my sister had to go through that. Then, once I did it…I couldn't make myself move past it."

I laughed humorlessly.

"You think you're the only one in pain, Reed?" I asked in a suspiciously calm voice. "Newsflash! You weren't!"

I was blaming my irrationality on the drugs that they were pumping into my system…or maybe my freakin' hormones were still whacked.

Whatever.

I didn't care.

My belly tightened as a sob hitched my throat, causing a shaft of pain to pour through me. Bile rose in my throat. I wanted to puke everywhere. But I knew I couldn't. This needed to be said, and if I started throwing up everywhere, he'd get all concerned. Then I wouldn't be able to get anything out of him because he was a freakin mother hen when it came to me. He always had been.

Which hurt even worse. He loved me. I loved him. But he refused to have anything to do with me because he thought it was the right thing to do. Or at least…he had been. Now, I didn't even know.

However, half his argument when we were younger had to do with my parents and how much he disliked them, and they disliked him.

Well, they weren't in the picture anymore, now were they?

"What are you talking about, Kris?"

He looked utterly confused. Heartbroken.

"I introduced Jay to Amy," I said so softly that nobody would hear but him. "It was at a volleyball game. I don't even know why she was there…Jay was there to watch me because my father dragged him along." I looked away from his piercing stare. "I wish I'd never done it."

He didn't reply.

I was about to tell him my most secret shame.

"And then I found out what he did," I whispered. "You know when someone is trying to get you to see how it would feel, and they say, 'Well, what would you think if it was your own sister?'"

He didn't nod. Didn't so much as twitch.

"Before he found your sister?" I choked out. "Yeah, he was doing *that* to me."

His eyes closed.

"You don't think I know what Amy was going through?" He swallowed, looking like I'd just punched him in the gut. I watched his Adam's apple bob with the movement. "It was me he used to victimize. Now I'm paying for my sins. For never telling a cop what he did to me."

Reed was taken from me. My babies were almost taken from me. My life was only hours away from slipping away. What was next?

"No."

Reed's one word sounded like it was ripped straight out of his gut.

I smiled, but it wasn't in humor. It was in self-defamation.

"I was happy."

His eyes flashed.

"When he stopped, it was because he had someone new to do that to. Your sister."

"What did he do?"

I could tell it pained him to ask. He didn't want to know. If he knew, then he couldn't deny it anymore.

"What didn't he do?"

Reed made a sound in his throat that sounded like he'd been stabbed in the heart.

I didn't waver.

"My mom knew he came into my bedroom because I told her," I whispered. "She knew that Jay liked to t-touch me."

"Did he rape you?"

Blunt. To the point.

It was killing him. He needed to know, but he didn't want to know at the same time.

He wanted to remain blissfully in the dark. But hell, didn't we all? Nobody wanted to know that bad shit happened to the people they loved.

And I knew Reed loved me. It was in his eyes. The same love that was in my own.

"He never got that in depth," I whispered. "It started a while before we met. Stopped when Jay started spending so much time at your house."

I knew why he stopped…now. Then, I hadn't. I'd just been happy that he had.

But Reed had never known, and now I could see the self-condemnation as he tried to come to terms with not being able to save me from it. Eventually, I would've worked up the courage to tell him, but even now, I hadn't wanted to say the words.

Saying the words made them more real.

"That's why you freaked out when I first touched you?" He swallowed. "When I touched you…that first time."

I looked away.

"I needed to see your face…and when you tried to turn out the lights, I might've had a flashback. But you calmed me down, turned on the lights, and let me see your face. From that moment on, I was never scared of you again."

I looked back toward him and wanted to run into his arms.

He was mad, though.

I could tell.

"I'm sorry for not telling you."

He looked up at the ceiling, not accepting my apology.

"If I'd have known…"

I laughed harshly.

"I'm glad you didn't," I said honestly. "Right when I'd worked up the courage to tell you…Jay died. Then you would've stayed, because you felt pity. I get it. But if you didn't want to stay, I didn't want you to stay. I wanted you to live your life, and be happy."

"That's the thing."

My eyes flashed up to his.

"What's the thing?"

"The thing is that I *wasn't* happy. Not even close. Tobias caught Jay…and then I got it in my head that I had to tell you goodbye. Kris, I haven't been happy since you walked out the door that day."

I wiped away the tears that were spilling down my cheeks.

"I guess that makes two of us." I sniffled. "But Reed…it's not enough. I want your love. Your time. Everything. I can't do this anymore. I need to either have all of you or none of you. This in between…I don't freakin' like it. It literally hurts me to be around you. So, you need to make a decision. You need to figure out whether you want me and the babies, or if we should make a visitation schedule where you can see them, but I won't be there."

"You think I don't love you?"

"A man doesn't stay away from the woman he loves."

I wanted to take the whispered words back before they'd even left my mouth, but now that they were out, I had to own up to the fact that they were true.

He gave me a kidney. He gave me half of his liver. He'd saved my life.

But saving someone's life didn't mean that you loved them.

Hell, people gave away kidneys all the time to a stranger. Sure, it's rare, but it happened.

I was tired.

I was worn out.

I felt like nothing ever got any easier.

I wanted to see my babies.

It fucking sucked that I still couldn't.

And I needed something more from Reed than just a shoulder to cry on.

I needed him to give me him.

To open up that steel-clad door and let me in.

And if he wasn't going to let me in, then I needed to let him go.

Because I couldn't do it anymore.

I needed something in my life to go right for once.

I needed Reed.

"You think I don't love you?" he laughed. "A man that doesn't love a woman would stay away from her. I can't stay away from you. If you get too far away, like when you went to fucking Germany, my heart palpitates. I can't function without knowing you're okay. So, I followed you."

I opened my mouth to speak, but he shut me up by placing a finger to my lips.

"My turn," he growled.

I bit my lip and leaned back in my new bed they'd transferred me into once I'd been let out of the ICU.

"What else?" he bit out as he got up out of his bed and started to pace. "I have parts on hand at Travis's shop for your car. If anything goes wrong with that piece of junk, I have the parts in stock on the shelf for Travis to fix it. I think I have a few headlight assemblies in my Amazon cart right now because I saw that one of them was acting up again."

My mouth fell open.

"I've been paying the old man that you bought your place from for ten years now. I didn't want him to sell it, but I didn't want to buy it, because you always said that you wanted to be there to sign the papers with me." He turned around and started walking back. "Vet visits for Pepe. I paid for those, too. It wasn't a kindness on their part since you adopted from one of their events. I made sure that I pre-paid. They still have my name on his records. That's why, when they called a few days ago, I didn't tell you who was on the phone. They were reminding me that Pepe had his annual check-up, and I didn't want to see you cry."

Because Pepe was dead.

Oh, God.

"Reed," I breathed.

"You want more proof that I love you?"

I closed my eyes and shook my head.

"I can't sleep. I don't think I've slept a full night since you left my house." He paused. "I followed you home. I made sure you got there safely, walking behind you in the rain. I saw you drop down onto your knees on your front lawn, and I dropped down on mine in the street."

A mewl left my mouth as I tried to hold my tears at bay.

It didn't work.

They coursed down my cheeks.

"One of the happiest days of my life was when you came in that clinic, and I found out that you were pregnant with my babies," he whispered gruffly. "The. Best."

Hot tears dropped from my chin onto my arm, but I didn't reach up to swipe them away.

There were too many at this point.

Nothing would stop them short of a freakin' towel.

"The second-best day of my life?" He cracked his knuckles. "Waking up from my drug-induced haze, and finding out that you made it through surgery."

I couldn't freakin' speak. Could hardly breathe.

"The third?" He leaned back against the wall across from me, kept his eyes on mine, and let me have it all. "The day you get to see the babies with me the first time."

"That hasn't happened yet." I hiccoughed.

He smiled. "But it will…soon. And when it does, that'll be my third best day."

A sob caught in my throat, and I suddenly couldn't stand for him to be so far away.

"Get in this bed with me."

The moment he did, and I was close enough, he wrapped his arms around me and held on tight.

Both of us hurt.

Both of us were uncomfortable.

But having him so close…well, nothing else would ever compare.

It was too tight, but I didn't mind.

What I did care about was that he was holding me. He was there. He was letting me in.

"I want to dig up his grave, and chop his bones up with a hacksaw. Burn them, and piss on them to put the fire out." He growled.

"You saved me," I whispered to him. "You don't know it, but you did. I was broken. And you and your love fixed me."

"I fucking hate him," he said. "I didn't think I could hate him even more, but somehow, I've managed it."

"It's okay. It's over," I lied.

It was never going to be okay. I was never going to forget. Not ever.

"Listen to me very carefully."

I shut up and listened, realizing that Reed wanted to speak, and wouldn't take no for an answer.

"Not a day has gone by in twelve years that I haven't thought about you. Wished that I'd made a different decision." He repositioned himself in the bed, and a painful grimace crossed his face. Before I could tell him to go to his own bed, he continued—and completely rocked my world in the process. "I want what he stole from us. The house. The land. The kids. You. If you would've died, I don't know what *I* would have done. I want to say that I would've done the adult thing and taken care of our kids. Made a life for them. And maybe I would have. Most likely, though, they wouldn't know the same man that you left. They'd know a shell of a man who didn't want to be in a world that you weren't a part of." His eyes were intense as he leaned forward. "I love you, Kris. Always have, and always will. There's nothing holding me back anymore. I don't care who doesn't approve. I don't care if my brothers will secretly hate it—even though they don't. I don't care if my mom never speaks to me again. Hell, I don't even have to live here if that's the case. All I care about is you and our little family. Please don't say no."

"Say no to what?"

"To me asking to marry you." I looked at him with wide eyes.

"Is that what you're doing?"

He grinned and lifted his hand—which held a diamond ring in the palm. It was small. And everything I'd ever wanted.

"I probably shouldn't tell you this, but I bought this six years ago during a moment of weakness. I saw it, and thought of you."

A tear dropped down my cheek, and a wave of exhaustion washed over me.

My eyes drooped.

"Maybe."

He started to laugh. "All right."

"I'll keep the ring, though. Think about it real hard."

He grunted and slid the ring on my finger. It was a perfect fit.

"Perfection."

I agreed wholeheartedly.

And when the machine beeped, indicating that he'd pressed my pain pump button, I smiled at him. "The nurse told me that only I was allowed to press that," I teased.

He winked and stood, looking somewhat pained as he did.

"I'm a doctor. I can do it. Nobody else, though."

I snorted. "Whatever."

He leaned forward so our foreheads touched.

I threaded my hands around his neck, lifted my face so my nose could rub against his, and said, "I love you, Reed Hail."

He shivered. "I love you, too, Krisney Shaw. Always have, always will."

***

1 week later

I was nervous as hell as they pushed me into the NICU—neonatal intensive care unit—instead of to my car as they released me from the hospital.

My belly was doing somersaults, and I prayed that they were really okay like Reed's family, as well as Hennessy, kept assuring me that they were.

"Do you think they're ugly?"

Reed looked over at me in confusion as he situated his mask into place. "They're our children. They're not ugly. At least not to us."

I started to crack up. "I guess what I meant to say is, do you think they look like they did on the ultrasound?"

"You mean alien-like?"

I nodded.

"Maybe," he admitted. "They're two weeks old, but that only makes them thirty-four weeks adjusted. They'd still have six-eight weeks to fatten up if they were still developing inside you. Since they're not, they likely look scrawny. Like you."

I snorted.

We literally knew nothing about our children.

Not their sizes when they were born. Not what color hair they had, or whether they were boys or girls. They were identical, that we knew. So, they were either both girls or both boys. But other than that, we knew nothing.

"Let's do this."

Reed pushed into the room backwards like he was heading into surgery, his gloved hands extended in front of him. Mask in place securely over his nose and mouth. His eyes, though.

They showed his fear.

He was just as nervous as me, but he was trying not to show it.

I walked through and came to a stop just inches inside the room.

It was overwhelming.

The overhead lights were dark. Machines were everywhere. Lights were blinking almost everywhere in a strobe-like effect. It was hot. And the crying. All of the babies sounded like they were crying.

The room itself was square, and huge infant incubators were taking up the majority of the room.

Ten in total.

Since this was a smaller county hospital, they didn't have individual rooms for the babies. No, they were all crammed into this one too-small space. There was a counter high station right inside the door, and one nurse was typing away on the computer, not even looking up.

My eyes went for the nurse that I'd seen come to my room twice over the last week that I'd been in the hospital.

She was standing in between two of the huge glass-domed beds, a chart in her hand.

I made my way to her, knowing with certainty that she was next to my children.

She had other babies, of course, but I just knew that they were mine.

Like a homing beacon was inside of me, guiding my way straight to my babies.

Every step I took caused a twinge. One in my belly. One in my side. One in my back.

It didn't matter, though.

Nothing did but meeting the babies that were mine.

Mine and Reed's.

My steps were slow, and Reed stayed at my side, keeping the same pace.

When we arrived at the woman, my eyes automatically skittered every which way.

There was too much to look at. Machines. Lights. Monitors. Papers hanging off the incubators.

My eyes focused on the nurse.

She was writing something down, and when I got closer, I realized that it said, 'Feeding Schedule' on the top in bold black letters.

"They eat a lot," I breathed, looking at all the times she'd written down.

The nurse smiled, and then gestured to the baby to her right. "This one just ate. I'm feeding baby B next!"

I looked over at baby A, and fell in love.

Tiny…so freakin' tiny.

The baby looked like a doll. Honest to God, if I didn't see the baby's chest rising and falling, I would've said it was one.

One of those tiny ones that look small, even in a toddler's arms.

"Oh, God," I breathed.

Reed's hand tightened at my hip.

I wanted to pick the baby up and cuddle it.

"You can't hold them yet," she murmured softly, reading my thoughts. "Their skin is like paper, and tears easily. You can touch them, though. Just be super careful."

I swallowed.

I didn't want that—their skin to tear.

Not at all.

"My mother happen to be here today?"

I blinked, surprised that I hadn't remembered that Reed's mother freakin' worked in the NICU.

"Not today, no. She works opposite shifts of me. So, when I'm here, she's not, and vice versa," the nurse, her name was Temperance, explained. "But she's gotten a lot of lovins in on these boys."

Boys.

Holy, *holy* shit.

"Boys?" I squeaked.

The nurse grinned. "Boys."

"Holy crap," I breathed. "You gave me two boys, Reed."

Reed was grinning ear to ear, and I could tell he was just as happy as I was.

Not that I didn't want a girl—eventually—I just had always seen us having boys first.

I moved to the incubator and peered in the side, my eyes taking everything in at once.

The lines running every which way. One attached to his foot with what looked like a Band-Aid. Another one attached to the left side of his chest, followed by another on the right. There was an IV line in the baby's head.

Oh, God.

His head.

I moaned.

Reed squeezed my hip again.

"You can do this if you'd like."

I looked at her over my shoulder, wondering what she wanted me to do.

"What?"

I'd do anything.

"Hold this right here." She gestured with her head to the tube cylinder she was holding. "It's the milk that he's eating for this hour."

Reed took the tube from her and gestured me forward.

I didn't want to leave the baby I was staring at, but I couldn't not do it.

I wanted to do it.

I moved to the other incubator.

The tube was nothing more than a syringe with the plunger part taken off. It was bigger than I'd seen, but not by much. It was also filled to the brim with milk.

"Do I just hold it?"

She nodded, as did Reed.

The moment my hand touched down on the plastic, I started to cry.

Reed's hand wrapped around me. After placing a kiss to my forehead, he gestured with his head to the other incubator. "I'm gonna go check out Bruiser over there."

I giggled, but was unable to take my eyes off of the baby boy on the white bed in front of me.

"Do you have to burp him?" I suddenly asked.

She shook her head, but it was Reed who answered me. "No. Since he's on a feeding tube, he's not sucking back air like a healthy baby would when they were eating. This one has your eyes. All slanted and angry."

I snorted and licked my lips.

I practically itched to press my lips to the little boy's tiny little nose.

This one…he looked like his daddy.

He had a head full of black hair, wide open grayish/blue eyes, and a nose that he'd have to one day grow into like his father had.

His hands were tiny…much smaller than anything I'd ever seen in my life. The entire little fist was about the size of a quarter.

His foot was about the size of a piece of Hershey's chocolate—the fun sized.

"Hey, baby," I whispered, my hand going to the glass just like I'd done with his brother.

"Do you have names for them yet?"

My eyes flicked up to Temperance.

"Uhh," I hesitated. "Kind of."

"Kind of?" she asked teasingly.

I nodded and looked over my shoulder at Reed.

"You tell her."

Reed chuckled.

This name thing had been hard as hell.

It'd taken us almost a month to name Pepe, and he was a puppy.

Naming a child was a huge commitment.

It'd taken us nearly two weeks of going back and forth over names before we found two that we adored.

"Do you want the D, or the B?"

I looked down at the baby that I was feeding.

"B."

"Baby A is Dash. Baby B is Bax."

Baxter and Dashiell. Both completely random names that we'd found in a baby book but had both liked.

"Love it," the nurse said. "I'll write that down in their charts. I'm only assuming this, but the last name is Hail, correct?"

She knew a little about us, I saw.

Momma Hail didn't completely hate me if she talked about me...*right?*

"Yes," I confirmed before Reed could. "We're getting married once the babies are out of here."

My absent-minded comment caused the man, who'd been talking quietly to his son, to stop speaking almost instantly.

I looked over my shoulder at him and saw he was watching me with excitement.

"You're saying yes?"

I laughed. "We'll see."

He growled. "I'll ask you right now."

I laughed. "I'm wearing your ring already, Reed. Asking me is only a formality at this point. I wanted to make you sweat."

"Well, you accomplished that," he muttered. "You done?"

I looked down at the syringe and saw that it was almost empty.

"Maybe?"

He left the baby he was standing near, and came to me, deftly removing the syringe and doing doctor things as I stared at our baby's face.

"You like this," I murmured.

He nodded. "The babies are my favorite part of my job." He paused. "I don't often interact with ones this small. I did do a few rotations in the NICU during my residency, though. If I ever had to pick a new specialty, this would be the place I'd go."

As I studied my baby, I suddenly blinked when I saw that he didn't have any eyebrows.

"He doesn't have any eyebrows!" I murmured.

"Or nails or eyelashes," Reed agreed. "Completely normal."

I looked, and indeed, he didn't have any fingernails or eyelashes, either.

"Holy shit," I murmured. "You're right."

He snorted. "I know."

A pitiful whine from behind me had me moving to the other bed, and I smiled when I saw Dash's head moving side to side.

"God, I want to hold you so bad," I murmured.

"You can touch him," the nurse, who I hadn't been aware was still there, said. "Just don't hold onto him."

I looked at my fingers, suddenly seeing weapons in my fingernails where before I would've seen just nails.

Carefully, I lifted one finger and ran it over the top of Dash's head.

"So soft," I murmured. "Like a little peach."

The nurse giggled. "Exactly like one," she agreed.

And so, it went.

Reed and I bounced between both kids until I was too exhausted to stand. When that happened, they found me a chair and I sat at Dash's bedside. Then moved ten minutes later to Baxter's.

Over and over until visiting hours ended.

When the new nurse, the night one, came in, everything literally stopped.

The parents that had been quietly looking at their own babies started to leave, and I realized that I was expected to go, also.

I wanted to cry.

Reed touched the tips of his fingers to my face, and then smiled knowingly.

"Let's go," he murmured. "We'll be back early."

We would.

I wouldn't have it any other way.

***

I hated leaving, but the NICU had strict policies that they adhered to when it came to visitors.

Not that I could complain. Those strict policies were protecting my two boys, and I wouldn't fault them for that.

"What now?" Reed asked.

Confused, I looked up to find him standing directly beside me, but his eyes were on the tall man that was leaning against the wall opposite of where we were exiting.

His eyes were hard, and surprisingly soft at the same time. As if he felt for what he was about to do.

"Do y'all have a minute?"

CHAPTER 19

Twatapotamus: a thing you're being right now.
-Text from Krisney to Reed

Reed

"Do y'all have a minute?"

I wanted to snarl that we didn't, but I knew that this couldn't be avoided any longer. I'd been putting him off for over a week to have his discussion with Krisney. It was time.

I'd given my family all the time I could. If they hadn't found Caria by now, it was time to involve the cops.

My eyes took in the detective.

He wasn't anyone that I knew, which meant he was probably new.

Which was a good thing seeing as Hostel hasn't had the best police department for years. Anything had to be better than what they had.

At one point, the entire police department had been put under investigation. They wouldn't have put a new guy in there unless he could prove himself.

I hoped.

"Kris," I murmured. "This is the detective over your case."

Krisney wasn't stupid. She was, in fact, rather smart when it came to life in general.

And she saw, just as well as I did, that this man wasn't the laid-back man he was trying to portray.

Then again, we'd both been active duty military for a while before we'd gone reserve. We weren't new to the game.

Krisney offered her hand to the detective, and then gestured toward a couple of seats at the end of the hall.

"I'm about to fall over," she admitted. "If I don't sit, I might fall."

The detective didn't even hesitate.

He let go of her hand and held his arm out for her to do what she needed to do.

Which made me proud of her.

I was happy that she wasn't trying to push her limits.

She'd just gotten released from the hospital earlier that morning. Technically she should've been at home, resting.

But I knew better.

At least this way I'd been able to keep an eye on her, and make sure that she didn't overdo it.

But now I wondered if I'd have to do that at all. The woman was so fucking smart that it hurt.

"Your fiancé is right," the detective said. "I'm the detective over your case. My name is Officer Cree, Tyler Cree."

"Nice to meet you," Krisney said as she sat.

The relieved look on her face made me wonder if I'd need to get a wheelchair for her to get to the truck with. The one she'd taken down here was gone the moment she got out of it.

"I wish we'd met under different circumstances." He paused. "How are the children?"

Krisney's smile lit up her entire face. "They're small, but they're fighting."

He nodded. "Good to know." He sighed and took a seat, the one opposite us, and started. "I want to know what happened. Do you have time…are you up for it?"

Kris looked down at her hands. "Where do you need me to start?"

"Start with how you met Caria."

Krisney looked at me.

"That would be where I come in, I suppose." I cleared my throat. "I started work here when Krisney was sixteen weeks pregnant. That was four months ago."

He nodded, his eyes on me. "Okay."

"Caria was already at the doctor's office when I started. We've had no relationship beyond that of co-workers whatsoever. There was one occasion when we went out to get coffee for the entire clinic, and another after I had just started, when we went out for lunch as a group with a few other members of the staff."

I could feel Krisney's eyes on me as I spoke, just as curious about my relationship with Caria as the detective was.

Krisney and I hadn't spoken much about anything after our surgeries. At least when it came to Caria, and why she did what she did.

Honestly, I wasn't too sure that I wanted to think about it.

If I thought about it, then I wanted to commit murder. And that was in direct violation of my oath as a doctor.

Surely there was an exception, though. One that said if she tried to murder the love of my life while she was pregnant with my children then she was allowed to get what was coming to her.

"I had no further involvement with her outside of work other than that one coffee run and the one group lunch," I told them both.

The same coffee run that I knew for a fact that Krisney had seen me while on. The one that had convinced me never to go anywhere alone with Caria again to do anything, no matter how much she begged me to go.

"Okay." Detective Cree nodded. "Tell me about your experiences with her."

A command, though put rather nicely, but still a command, nonetheless.

"I didn't have much of any relationship with her. I barely ever saw her other than at the office, and all of those times were never alone. The other nurse, Opal, who is Reed's personal nurse, was with her ninety nine percent of the time. The other one percent, Reed was with her."

"Opal is my nurse, and not a suspect from what I can tell," I told him. "She's the one who goes with me to the hospital and helps me by performing vitals, like blood pressures, reading results, sitting in on exams and is basically my right hand."

He nodded. "We've cleared Opal, as well as others in the office. They all corroborate your story."

"It's not really a story," Krisney admitted. "It's the truth."

He nodded. "Then they've corroborated your truth."

She nodded.

"Tell me about the day she gave you the oil."

So Krisney did, recounting everything that happened, including waking up later that night, scared to death.

"Pennyroyal, you say?"

I nodded. "Pennyroyal."

"I'll have to research that," he said. "Dr. Torres, as well as the lab, explained that this was detrimental to pregnancy."

"Not only pregnancy, but yes," I said. "Very dangerous."

Detective Cree pulled out a tiny notebook from his left breast pocket.

"I have two more things," he said, flipping through the pages. "Are either one of you aware that Caria tried to buy the property that Krisney now owns?"

Krisney's mouth dropped open in surprise.

Mine didn't.

I'd known that almost a year ago.

I hadn't put two and two together, though, until much more recently.

"I blocked her from buying the property," I admitted. "Apparently her family had owned it at one point. Her grandfather wouldn't sell it to her, though. His family blocked his wishes for how his wife was to be buried, and he hadn't talked to them since. When I came along a few years later, I started paying the taxes on his land, as well as 'rent' as you could say." I looked at Krisney. "I don't know how much of our relationship you know, but we were high school/college sweethearts."

He nodded. "We had a tragedy occur in my family, and we broke up."

He nodded again.

Krisney made a weird noise in her throat, making me wince.

"Anyway, that property was by the apartment complex where I used to live during the time we were together. It meant a lot to us, and I wanted to make sure that it was there if she ever moved back home."

Detective Cree blinked.

"How did you know that Caria wanted the property?"

"The owner told me. He explained that he was struggling financially and that he was going to have to sell. I paid him ten grand not to, and he was happy to do that, because again, like I said, he disliked that entire side of his family for putting him into a bad position during such a hard time in his life."

Cree watched me, and then sighed.

"Did you know that Caria was in the same school as you, Reed?"

"High school or college?" I asked in confusion.

"Required classes in college..." he pulled up the paper. "Both of you were in the same biology, microbiology, statistics, calculus..."

I held up my hand. "Okay."

"I guess what I'm trying to say is that she's likely had you on her radar for a very long time," he paused and looked at Kris. "From what I've been able to gather from looking into her background, she's always been mentally unstable."

"Great," Krisney mumbled under her breath.

Cree's mouth kicked up at the corner. "She spent two years in a self-imposed psychiatric ward because she said she heard voices telling her to harm other people. Since the institution was privately funded and staffed to maintain the highest levels of patient confidentiality, her nursing background check didn't pick up that she was institutionalized."

I growled under my breath.

"I'm not sure when she started to become obsessed with you, but either of those two times would be my guess." He paused. "Had y'all been together," he looked between the two of us, "when she first caught sight of Reed, my guess would be that she would've done this a whole hell of a lot sooner than she did."

"Where is she?"

Cree didn't say anything for a very long moment, and I knew without him saying that he didn't know.

"We haven't been able to locate her," he admitted. I also didn't admit that my family hadn't, either. "We've gone through her apartment, got the super to let us into her place. Found her clothes gone, and that's it. She's hiding."

Rafe had said much the same. Him, Travis, and Baylor, as well as Baylor's friend Parker who was recently hired, had done a lot of investigating on their own. Caria was nowhere to be found.

"She knows that I'll fuck her up if I ever see her again," I mumbled under my breath.

Krisney punched me gently on the arm. "Now that's not any way for a doctor to talk."

I chuckled, the hard rasp of it tickling the back of my throat.

I honestly didn't give one flying fuck how a doctor was supposed to 'talk.' What I gave a fuck about was the fact that she'd tried to take everything away from me just because I wasn't paying her any attention.

"What now?" I asked.

Detective Cree replaced his notebook before saying, "We wait for her to come out of hiding. There's nothing we can do until she makes another appearance."

I saw red.

"You want to give her another chance to do what she couldn't last time?"

Detective Cree looked me dead in the eye and said, "She can try..."

He didn't have to finish that sentence.

He wouldn't let her get that far.

"You're watching us?"

He nodded. "As is half the town, to be honest." He looked between the two of us. "And don't think I don't notice those repo-boys of yours. Two of them aren't as obvious as the other two, but I know they're doing it. Not to mention y'all are the town's 'golden' couple." He tilted his head slightly. "I've heard from quite a few people that y'all were the couple that everyone was rooting for. Once y'all finally got back together, they were none too happy to find out that the relationship had been threatened." He stood up to leave. "Plus, your brothers have been working with me, as well as Raphael, after a little persuasion."

"Who's Raphael?" Krisney asked.

"Rafe," I said at the same time that Detective Cree said, "Raphael Luis, he works with Dante."

My eyebrows rose at the way he said 'works.'

He didn't sound like he believed that Rafe was actually working.

"You know Rafe?" I questioned him.

Detective Cree nodded once. "Yep. He and I used to be in the military together."

The way he said it, though, made it sound like he was unwilling to say anything more than what he'd said. Which meant I shut the hell up about it, because although Cree had been helpful and somewhat careful with Krisney today, being mindful of her delicate nature, I didn't for one second forget that the man wasn't anybody that I knew.

I didn't know him from a random Joe I met at the grocery store.

But if he knew Rafe, then that meant that he had to be vouched for, at least partially.

If Rafe didn't like him, I would've already heard.

Rafe was weird like that, though.

A couple of months ago, I'd found out that although he was working for Travis, he was also down here on his own agenda, helping set up safe houses for a corporation out of Kilgore that helped rescue abused women.

Rafe also knew shit that nobody else knew.

However, I never knew when he was going to pop up.

I trusted him with my life, though.

And now, those of my children.

I offered Cree my hand, and he took it.

"Congratulations on the children."

I shook it and let it go before answering. "Thank you."

With that parting comment, he left, leaving Krisney and I staring at each other.

"I won't let her hurt you or the children again," I promised.

She smiled sadly. "I never said you would."

CHAPTER 20

*Not only did I fall off the diet wagon, it rolled over on top of me
and forced me to eat its contents.
-Krisney's secret thoughts*

Krisney

After leaving the hospital, we headed to eat at my favorite place in
the world—Roadhouse.

I had an irrational love for it.

It was always there when I needed it, and when I was away on
deployment, or during those god-awful years where I lived with
my parents in Alabama, I'd missed the place.

Now, every time I was near it—which admittedly wasn't often
since it was thirty minutes away from Hostel where I lived—I ate
there.

"I called your boss," Reed said out of the blue as we pulled into the
parking spot right in front of the door.

My brows rose. "Why?"

"I wanted him to know what was going on." He bit his lip. "I also
should've mentioned it before, but he'd technically already fired
you when you hadn't shown up for two weeks of work. He never
put two and two together since he's the new dentist in town. He
didn't realize that you were the one who had to have emergency
surgery, until I'd called him. I'm sorry I didn't call sooner, but it
slipped my mind."

I started to laugh, which I immediately regretted.

Everything hurt.

The pain medication they'd given me earlier in the day before I'd been discharged from the hospital had worn off, and now I was feeling every single bit of the pain that was radiating through my body.

I definitely needed some of my pain medication.

"Let's go inside so I have something to wash a pain pill down," I replied quietly.

Reed frowned. "You're hurting?"

I pushed open the door and steeled myself for the pain I knew was going to roll over me after I stood up, and nearly moaned when it did.

Though it'd been two weeks since my surgery, everything still hurt. Which, apparently, was normal.

My also new normal: pills. Lots of them. Anti-rejection pills at the top of that list.

I, on the other hand, thought that 'normal' sucked.

That, and I didn't want to go home.

I didn't want to be alone.

I didn't want to be in a house without my children. Without Reed.

So, I was stalling by telling him I was starving and wanted to go to a restaurant that I knew I wasn't quite ready for this soon after getting out of the hospital.

I shuffled inside, though, pain pill bottle clutched tightly in my hand as I did.

He arrived at my side, seeming much more at ease than I was, despite having his freakin' kidney and half a liver removed. One would think that getting a kidney and a half of a liver would be easier.

Let me tell you something: it isn't.

Though mine had been 'more in depth' he'd said, I still didn't think that they were all that much different. Though, I wouldn't let him go into detail. There was only so much I could take, and hearing him get all medical on me wasn't one of those things.

However, I had had a C-section on top of the rest of my surgeries—IE my liver and kidney transplant.

My liver and kidney that used to be in Reed's body.

I did a full body shiver, and he looked at me worriedly.

"You think they'll give us a booth?" I asked, trying to distract him.

They did.

And two baskets of rolls—rolls that I asked for when she tried to skimp on us by only giving us three of them.

"Oh, and extra butter!"

The hostess who routed us to our table and gave us our first basket of rolls looked at me oddly.

"I just had two babies. I haven't had this much room inside of me for a long time," I told her defensively.

She grinned.

"How long ago?" she idly chit-chatted.

My belly clenched. "Two weeks."

"First time out on a date with baby daddy without them?" She smiled. "I remember that time. I was so scared to leave my little girl at home with my mom, but my ex-boyfriend practically begged me to go eat with him. So, I did. It was the most miserable two hours of my life."

I looked away.

I didn't have a choice on whether to be away from them.

I didn't reply to her, and when I felt Reed's squeeze on my lower hip, I knew he felt much the same way.

Neither one of us wanted to be away, and we both knew it.

We put on a brave face, though.

Talked about what we needed to buy at the store for our children, and overall, had an excellent time sitting in a restaurant with each other.

It was like old times again. Such a surreal feeling that I wasn't sure if I could trust the feeling inside of me—semi-contentment.

And I say semi because what would've made it perfect would have been to have our children at home with us. Safe, sound and within arm's reach.

But we didn't have that and wouldn't for a while.

"How long do you think they'll be in the NICU for?"

His eyes took me in.

"If we're lucky? Two months. They'll want the babies to get to five pounds. That's hospital protocol. Some hospitals do four, but I agree with five. Five means that they're more fully able to regulate their body heat, and that they have a better chance of survival outside of a hospital setting."

My stomach clenched.

"Do you think they'll be okay?"

His eyes searched mine, and I knew right then and there that he was trying to decide how much to tell me of what he wanted to say.

"Just be honest," I ordered.

His smile was small.

"Okay." He paused. "What I think is that they started off on the wrong foot with what Caria did to you. They're monitoring their liver and kidney functions twenty-four seven. They're trying to make sure that nothing happened to affect them with the oil that she gave you. Since we don't know much about the plant, we don't have much more than a basic understanding of the effects it will have on unborn children—and children who are now out of the womb."

I looked down at my hands as a wave of sickness washed over me.

I'd done this to them.

"But, overall, their tests are looking good. They're two weeks old, and both are doing well considering their age." He cleared his throat, causing me to look up at him. "Will this be an easy road for them? No. It'll probably be one of the hardest things they'll ever have to do, and they won't even know it."

I blinked back a tear.

"But they're our babies. They're fighters. There's not one second that I think they'll forget to fight. And in the end, I think we'll be taking home two healthy babies."

I breathed out shakily.

"I'm so scared."

"What can I get y'all to drink?" the waitress, who magically appeared at the side of the table, asked.

"Couple sweet teas, please," I murmured, smiling.

"Any appetizers?"

I looked down at the rolls that didn't seem the least bit appetizing any longer and shook my head. "No."

She left without another word, and I looked back at my soon-to-be husband.

"You know that you don't have anything to be scared about."

I grinned. "Not yet."

He was right.

I didn't have any reason to be scared.

After hearing the conversation with the detective earlier, knowing that everyone was keeping an eye on us, I knew that Caria wouldn't be able to get to us. She'd be left with no other choice but to either confront us physically despite the presence of people looking out for us, or leave us alone.

Since I knew she wouldn't be leaving us alone, I just had to wait for her to make her appearance.

And when she did, I'd slam her head into the floor for what she did to me so carelessly.

"That face you just made is hot," Reed said, making me grin.

"Yeah," I murmured, reaching for a roll just as our teas were placed in front of us.

After ordering, I went back to staring at Reed.

"What did you just ask her?" I questioned.

"I was asking where the bathroom was."

I nodded. "Behind me, remember?"

He looked up, then started to laugh. "Guess I didn't see that flashing neon 'restroom' sign."

I snorted.

"Speaking of," I said. "I gotta go."

"Call out if you fall in."

I flipped him the bird and went to stand, only to come to a halt when waiters of every shape and size started to crowd around me.

"Attention, Texas Roadhouse!"

He pretended it was my birthday.

That had been the whispered conversation.

Why? Because he thought it was funny.

It wasn't. But he laughed, so I didn't throw a fit because I liked seeing him smile.

"Happy birthday dear Krisney. Happy birthday to you."

It took them three embarrassing minutes to leave, and thankfully, since I was still moving slow, they didn't make me straddle the booth like I'd seen them do the last time I'd dined there.

"Why?" I asked furiously, staring at the free cake that was now sitting in my spot.

He smiled.

"Because instead of being an ass every single time I saw you, I should've told you I loved you. Instead of going out of my way to ignore your presence, I should have kissed you. Instead of missing your birthday dinner for the last decade, I should have celebrated with you."

CHAPTER 21

No thanks, mall. I shop at home without pants like a normal person.
-Text from Krisney to Reed

Reed

"Do you want to go home and get a change of clothes?"

She looked at me like I'd grown a second head.

"What?"

"Do you want to…"

She stopped me with a lifted hand. "I know what you said. Why would I need a change of clothes?"

"Because you're staying at my place." I blinked. "I mean, you can wear my clothes all you want, I just figured we'd go straight to the hospital from my place once we woke up, and visiting hours opened up."

She blinked.

"You want me to stay with you?"

I tilted my head. "You don't want to stay with me?"

The sheer panic I felt at her staying somewhere without me was wholly terrifying.

She tilted her head in confusion. "Reed, you didn't ask me, and I didn't want to assume."

I closed the door to her side of the truck and rounded the vehicle, the pain and tiredness I was feeling getting the upper hand.

I most certainly didn't think I could make it through the rest of the days without her in the bed lying right beside me like the night before.

"You're staying," I said. "I don't want to hear any lip."

She just shook her head, unable to form words.

"What time do you want to head out in the morning?" I asked as I got into my seat, closed the door, buckled myself in, and started the truck.

She grinned. "I want to get there the moment they open the doors, of course."

I snorted. "I'm glad you feel the same way I do."

What I thought was going to be an awkward drive turned out to be quite entertaining as we tried to decide who they looked like more.

Mostly we decided that my genes were dominant seeing as they both had my facial structure, dimpled chin and blue eyes.

The only features that seemed to be Krisney's on both children were their heart-shaped mouths.

By the time we arrived at the house, we'd spoken non-stop for a whole five minutes, and there hadn't been a single awkward pause.

At least not until we pulled into the driveway and saw my brother, Dante, as well as Rafe standing there.

Dante was a surprise.

He'd been making himself scarce after an accident had claimed the lives of his children and wife—an accident that had been caused by our sister.

I couldn't blame him for his withdrawal, though. I'd almost experienced that myself just a couple short weeks ago, and just living a few hours of my life thinking that Krisney wouldn't be in it for much longer had felt like I'd been repeatedly punched in the chest.

How Dante lived it, day in and day out, was a phenomenon to me.

"Dante," Krisney breathed.

I looked over at her as I shut the truck off.

"That's his daughter," I murmured.

Dante was holding his child—a little girl by a woman who was no longer in the picture—and staring at us through the windshield of my truck.

"Hmmm?" she breathed.

"Nobody told you *that* particular little tidbit?"

She didn't answer, completely forgetting the box of leftovers that she'd insisted we bring home.

She climbed out and then shuffled the length of the driveway that separated her from Dante, walking straight up to him and wrapping her arms around him.

My breath caught in my throat at the sight.

Dante looked broken all over again for a few long seconds as he held Krisney closely, and then patted her gently on the upper back, whispering something softly in her ear as he did.

The jealousy that I would've felt with any other one of my brothers wasn't there. All that was there was a sense of hope. A tiny little flicker as I hoped and prayed that maybe, just maybe, Dante was healing. And when he was done healing, he would come back to us.

The moment was there and gone in less time than it would take to recite the alphabet, but the hope that was taking root in me, despite the perilous situation we were in, was enough to make me feel happy.

"I had your place wired."

I looked up to find Rafe staring at me expectantly.

"Thanks?"

He snorted.

"I had a guy install it. Came down from Kilgore to do it. He's going to be monitoring this off site, and any problems that he sees while he's monitoring it, he'll forward straight to the police department, Detective Cree's phone, as well as mine and your brothers."

I blinked.

"So, I have nannies?"

Rafe shrugged.

"If that's how you want to look at it," he shrugged.

My eyes narrowed.

"What are you really doing here?" I asked. "You're not here because you're working for my brother and need a job."

His eyes held mine. "No, I'm not."

I growled.

"Rafe…"

"Rafe can't talk to you, just like he can't talk to the rest of us. When it's done, he'll be leaving. Until then, just let him do what he does best."

"And what the fuck is that?"

Krisney placed her hand on my chest, and all anger fled.

I didn't even know why I was mad.

I just knew that I had to be mad at someone, and both of the men standing in front of me were convenient targets.

"I don't have the answers you're looking for right now," Dante said. "But when I do, you'll know."

Which pretty much meant he had some information that he wasn't willing or able to share.

Typical Dante.

"Whatever," I muttered. "Can you at least tell me what it has to do with Caria, Krisney and me?"

"That," Dante said, "has nothing to do with him. Rafe is here for a completely different reason." He paused. "He's just willing to help out while he's here when he has some downtime."

Rafe looked like he would've added more, but the little girl in my brother's arms—my niece—stirred.

She was a little bit of a thing—or at least I'd have thought that before I'd met *my* children.

Dante started to bounce her, but Krisney put her hand on his forearm. "If I go inside, can I hold her? Let y'all talk for a minute?"

Dante looked like he was reluctant to give her up, but he nodded once and followed her inside, leaving Rafe and me alone long enough that I could say a few words.

"If my brother's in trouble, I want to know."

Rafe nodded once.

"Is he?"

Rafe's eyes studied me.

"Not yet," he said. "But he's right. I don't have any information. Not any more than when I came here. But I'll find it."

With that he disappeared into the shadows until he blended in with the night.

"Rafe leave?"

I looked over my shoulder at Dante. "Yeah."

"Did he tell you anything?"

I looked at my brother, studying how he'd changed over the last year.

He was harder. Darker. Less receptive to talking.

It was funny, really.

Dante was the big brother. The protector.

Now he looked like a man possessed. Like something was on the tip of his tongue, and he was about to let the whole fuckin' world have it.

And honestly? Maybe he was.

Maybe he was going to fuck everybody up, and it was only a matter of time.

"Why are you looking at me like that?" he barked.

"Yes," I answered his earlier question. "He told me this whole sordid tale that centers around you and everything—everyone—that you've decided to hurt."

His eyes flashed for a moment, as if I'd hit home with those few pointed words, but just as suddenly as it appeared it was gone.

"Rafe didn't tell you anything." he snorted. "Not if he wants to fuckin' live, anyway."

I tilted my head and stared at him.

"What are you doing here, Dante?"

He turned his head and studied the darkened street where Rafe had disappeared.

"It's time."

"It's time for what?"

"To return to the land of the living."

"Why?"

I had a feeling it had a lot to do with the little girl that was currently inside with Krisney.

The little girl that we only got to see once in a blue fucking moon—IE, when one of us brothers got hurt.

Tobias. Travis. Baylor. Me.

"Because I have some unfinished business."

"What kind of unfinished business?"

"The kind that I don't want to talk about right now," he amended. "But when I do, you'll be the first to know."

I growled.

"Dante, that's bullshit, and you know it."

He looked away.

"It's got nothing to do with you, and everything to do with me." He took a deep breath. "I…it's a mistake I'm rectifying. Once I have it all figured out…I'll be back."

"You'll be back," I repeated. "Why? How?"

"Sometimes the darkness hurts," he whispered. "I'm…fucking tired of seeing only black. I want to see sunshine again. I want to be a better person. Mary needs me to dig my way out, and that's what I'm doing."

I didn't know what to say to that.

"I need a favor, though." He returned his gaze to me.

"Anything."

I didn't even hesitate.

I could tell I surprised him, causing me to grin.

That grin quickly fell with what he had to say next.

"If I die…"

"Dante…"

He held up his hand to stop me from speaking.

"If I die, you have to take care of Mary."

"You know I will," I said. "We all will."

He nodded once. "I need to go…just remember one thing."

I waited for him to say what he had to say, and immediately regretted letting him say it.

"You're stronger than what you think. I've always admired you." He looked at his hands. "Don't let her go. Don't waste even a second." He took in a shaky breath. "Don't be like me. Don't take one single freakin' second for granted…because sometimes they don't make it home like you're expecting them to. Sometimes life rips your soul to shreds and then expects you to go on living as if your heart wasn't just ripped right out of your chest."

I closed my eyes.

"Don't waste it."

***

"I used to babysit a little girl who had Down Syndrome," Krisney said softly.

My eyes were wide open as I replayed what Dante had said to me an hour before.

After Dante had collected his sleeping little girl from my fiancée's arms, he'd walked out of the door and straight to his truck without another word.

An old company vehicle. One that I hadn't seen in a while.

The one and only time I'd seen him out and about after the accident that had taken his wife and kids—as well as his car—he had been on a motorcycle. He still had his wife's car parked in his garage, but I knew he wouldn't drive it. Not ever again.

Hence the old company tow truck.

He could put the little girl into a car seat in the back seat.

"Oh yeah?" I murmured.

"She was the sweetest, kindest, most beautiful little girl that I ever met," she whispered into the darkness. "She gave the best hugs, and I adored her from the tips of her piggy tails to her pink little toenails."

"She sounds like a sweet little girl."

"She was," she agreed. "But…Reed, that little girl absolutely adored everyone and everything. Unfortunately, the reverse wasn't true for her."

"What do you mean?"

"I mean," she cleared her throat. "That Mary, Dante's daughter, has a tough road ahead of her. Not everyone is as accepting as we are, and one day, Mary's going to be the target of some hate. I just hope when that day comes, that Dante doesn't go off on some ignorant teenager who may be acting like a jerk but isn't really a bad person."

I grunted.

"Dante…" I growled. "Well, he's getting there."

"Why now?"

"Mary."

She rolled over slowly until she was pressed to my side.

My chest felt like it warmed fifteen degrees just by the simplest of touches.

I knew she wasn't comfortable, but I could feel her determination to stay there.

"I…I'm…I wish I was there for you when that happened."

I didn't say anything for a long moment as I tried to collect my thoughts.

"Do you want to know my worst days?"

She froze.

"I want to know everything you're willing to tell me," she finally said.

"The day that we lost Dante's family and then realized that it was Amy's fault. The day that we buried Dante's family. The day that Amy died. The day that we buried her." I paused. "But, those were nothing compared to the day that I told you to leave."

"That day, I knew I'd fucked up." I laughed harshly. "Amy told me I was stupid. Did you know that?"

I felt a tear hit my arm, and I knew what I told her, and the memories they brought, caused her to cry.

"No," she cleared her throat.

"She did," I said. "She told me that I was a dumb person, and that one day I was going to regret telling you to leave."

I laughed harshly. "What she didn't know is that I regretted those words as I was saying them."

"Reed," she breathed.

"Used to pray for sleep, because that was the only place that my life didn't suck. That was the only place where I got to see you."

She sniffled and rubbed her nose along the skin of my arm.

"Reed," she tried to interrupt.

"Couldn't fucking wait to lay my head on the pillow at night," I continued. "I used to think about you all day long, and it felt like a freakin' anvil was sitting on my chest. In my dreams, though, you were there. You were happy. I was happy. We got to live our lives together and live our happily ever after."

"Reed, we'll have that."

I started to say more, but she raised her hand and put it against my mouth. "No more talking."

I smiled against her hand.

"Yes, ma'am."

"You bet yes, ma'am," she countered.

I placed a gentle kiss on her palm and then urged her to roll onto her back.

"Go to sleep, Krisney."

"Bossy," she said.

"Determined," I countered. "Worried. Scared. In love."

"You have such pretty words."

"They're the whole truth, and nothing but the truth, so help me God."

She settled on her back, propped up partially with a pillow to keep her off the side with the incision, and then reached down for my hand.

"This time, your dreams are going to be nothing compared to your reality."

I had no doubt that they would be.

"And Reed?"

"Yeah?" I asked, sleep starting to pull me under.

"I don't hate you. I never have and never will."

That was good, because I hated myself enough for the both of us.

CHAPTER 22

I often times try to convince myself that I actually like people. Then I go to the grocery store at five o'clock and realize that I'm fooling myself.
-Krisney's secret thoughts

Krisney

We'd both forgotten our cell phones at home.

Last night, after all that had gone on with Dante, we completely forgot to plug them in to charge, so of course they both were dead.

After a restless first night at home where neither of us slept well, we plugged our phones in to charge while we got dressed. But we had been in such a rush to leave that we forgot to grab them

It wasn't until we had arrived at the hospital that Reed had realized our mistake.

"I have to go back and get them," he said. "Everyone will freak if they can't get a hold of us."

I agreed.

"Okay," I said, getting out of the car. Slowly. "I'll start making my way up. You might catch me before I even get up there."

He grinned. "You're not that slow, but I'll try to be quick." He looked at me sternly. "And when you get there, make sure you find a chair. Don't stand up the entire time I'm gone."

I saluted him, causing his eyes to light with humor. "Be good."

"Don't forget the charger. They're probably not fully charged yet, but I'm sure they have somewhere we can plug them in here."

He winked and was gone, leaving me at the entrance staring at his truck driving away.

When I arrived on the NICU floor, I wasn't prepared for the flurry of activity in the room.

"What's going on?" I asked another one of the parents.

The mom looked tired, run down and scared.

"One of the babies stopped breathing and another followed shortly after," she said. "When that happens, all of the parents have to leave."

"Whose babies?" I blurted.

I didn't have to guess who, though.

I could see that all the activity was centered around the two incubators in the back right corner of the room.

The exact same corner where Reed and I had spent nearly five hours yesterday after I'd been released from the hospital.

Reed had turned around to go get our phones, and now I was left standing here, watching my worst nightmare playing out in front of me.

"Are you okay?"

"Those are my babies," I whispered.

The mother looked sad. Horrified.

"Oh, honey."

I walked up to the glass and rested my head there, staring at what was happening.

I couldn't think. Couldn't breathe.

Turning on my heel, I rushed as fast as I could make my body go, ending up in a deserted hallway with only a door leading to the stairs at the end of it.

I pushed through the stairwell door, climbed up a flight of steps, and tried not to cry from both the physical and emotional pain.

"I thought you'd never come."

I blinked, looked up, and came face-to-face with the woman who had nearly ruined my life.

The woman who was responsible for every awful thing that had happened to me over the last two weeks.

"You."

Caria smiled.

"Me."

I didn't know what to say.

Didn't know what to do.

Mainly because Caria had a fucking gun pointed at me, and I wanted to reach forward and yank her off the landing above me by her hair.

Then my stupid mouth took off before I could get it under control.

"You stupid, no good whore!" I screeched.

The deep breath I'd had to take made pain in my stomach and back explode, but it didn't stop me from saying the words.

Mainly because Caria was a stupid whore, and she needed to hear them.

"Touchy," she said as she cocked the hammer and then leaned forward. "Scream like that again, though, and I'll have to use this."

She waved the gun for emphasis.

I clamped my jaw shut and tried not to think about how my legs were starting to shake.

Not because she was scaring me—though she was—but because I still wasn't at full strength yet.

Which reminded me that my babies were currently fighting for their lives.

"You know," Caria smiled. "My badge still works. Still gets me into the hospital, and in locked places where I technically 'shouldn't' be."

Her smile was so fucking smug that I wanted to slap it off of her face.

"And since I worked on the baby floors, they freak out when you take kids out of the hospital." She laughed. "But, I just took the stupid bracelet off. I don't understand why they never thought of that. The sensors are good and all, but only if you leave them on their ankles. They're so easy to take off that it's almost comical, though."

I had no clue what she was talking about. None at all.

"Did you know they have a healthy set of twins on the maternity floor?"

I wanted to cunt punch her.

"Unlike you." Caria grinned, showing a row of perfectly white teeth.

I wanted to see those white teeth scattered on the floor after I slammed her head into the concrete a couple of hundred times.

"Unfortunately, they'd taken the boy of the twin set to go get his wiener skin chopped off—which might I add is a barbaric practice. I hate seeing circumcised men nowadays. So anyway, I had to find another."

I shouldn't have said it. I knew it, yet it came out anyway.

"You probably wouldn't like Reed all that much then," I told her. "He's circumcised. It doesn't affect the feeling in his dick at all, though. I'd say he's perfectly functional down there."

Caria screamed an inhuman scream and came down two steps, leaving the bag that'd been at her side on the landing.

Something was off about it.

Was it moving?

Before I could so much as glance at it, though, Caria came down two more steps.

"You think you're cute, don't you?" She sneered. "Well, let me tell you something." She took another step. "You're not."

And she swung her right fist at my face.

I ducked, but once I was down, I couldn't get back up.

***

Reed

I couldn't wait to stop feeling those twinges that would remind me that I wasn't in the top shape that I used to be.

I would be one day, though.

And wouldn't be winded by climbing a simple flight of stairs.

Well, technically, it was two flights. Ten stairs a piece that led to the second level. Twenty total.

There'd been a power surge of some kind that had caused the left bank of elevators that led to the floors above to stop working. That meant that the right bank of elevators was backed up with people waiting to get on it.

Anxious to get to Krisney and the boys, this delay led to me taking the freakin' stairs when I didn't really want anything to do with them for the time being.

I used to take these stairs in a flash as I made my way into the hospital and up to the labor and delivery floor. Now I was taking them so slow that I was sure I looked like an old man.

"Oh, man." I groaned.

The pinch was setting into a prominent twinge, which was what caused me to pause at the top of the first flight of stairs and take a short breather.

My eyes were trained ahead as I looked up at the number two painted on the wall above my head when I heard the screams.

"You stupid, no good whore!"

My head tilted to the side, and I leaned over the stairs to look up.

I couldn't see anything.

I could hear voices, though.

The voice sounded familiar, but with the way that the stairwell contorted voices, I couldn't even begin to tell you who, or what floor they were even on.

I started up to the next landing, the voices getting louder, and paused when my phone vibrated in my pocket.

I reached in and pulled it out, seeing that it wasn't my phone, but Krisney's.

I pressed the green accept button and put it to my ear just as another screech rent the air.

I leaned over the stairwell again, looked up, and immediately brought my head in just in time for a body to come flying over the stairwell.

The body screamed on her way down—and it was a her because I could see her long hair streaming upwards as she fell—to the ground at basement level.

My mouth fell open.

"Holy shit," I breathed, the phone to my ear.

"Krisney?" the woman on the other end of the line said.

"Uh, no," I said. "This is her fiancé, Reed. Mom?"

I didn't know what to do.

The minute that my mom asked for Krisney, I knew that she was working. The other nurse had said she worked opposite shifts from my mother, meaning that my mom was there. Where Krisney should be…

"Reed," my mother breathed.

I looked down at the body that was writhing two floors below, then up, still seeing nothing.

I climbed two sets of stairs, my suspicions getting to the point of screaming inside of me.

"The babies both had bouts of apnea today," she said, making my foot stall on the third floor. "Both of their lungs collapsed. The right one on Baxter, and the left one on Dash."

At the same time?

My eyes went up, and I froze.

Krisney was down on the ground, crying.

Her eyes met mine.

I looked over the landing again and studied the woman on the ground.

Caria.

My eyes flicked back up to Krisney.

"Are they okay?" I rasped.

There was so much going on that I didn't know what to do. Who to go to first.

One part of me was wanting to run up to Krisney, while the other wanted to run down to the NICU where my babies were. The other, and this was a very minute part, wanted to go all the way down the flight of stairs and see to the woman—Caria—who had fallen.

"We were able to get the lungs reinflated…" she paused. "You know that this is pretty common in premies, correct?"

"Yes," I croaked.

What else was common in ones so young? Brain bleeds. Digestive problems. Mental delays.

The list went on and on and on, and I had tried really hard not to think about that. To think about the fact that these babies had such a hard road in front of them.

"Okay," she said. "Today, they're restricting visitation due to the problems, but I'll keep you updated, and let you know if anything else goes wrong, okay?"

"Yeah, Mom." I croaked. "Thank you."

She hung up, and immediately I got a text from her, but I didn't have time to look at it.

After shoving the phone back into my pocket, I took the last eight steps that led me to Krisney, and looked down at her.

"Kris…"

"She had a gun."

"What?"

Krisney gestured to the side where Caria had plunged down from, but her eyes were on the bag that was two steps up on the landing.

"She had a gun." Then she tilted her head. "Reed, I think there's something alive in that bag."

The bag was one of those boho bags that crossed over the shoulder. A huge monstrosity that did appear to be moving.

"What the fuck?"

"Go look."

I reached into my pocket and handed her the phone. "Call 911."

"Were you talking to your mother?"

"Yeah," I croaked. "The babies…their lungs collapsed. Mom said that they're okay now, stable. But they're restricting visitation for today until they can be sure that they really are stable before letting us in."

Her head dropped. "I was so scared. That's why I'm in here…Reed, I think that she was on her way to the NICU floor. I don't know what she was going to do, but I feel like she was headed to our babies."

I didn't know what to say to that, so I continued to make my way to the bag.

"She didn't make it," I growled, then dropped down on one knee to look into the bag.

My heart literally stalled in my chest when I saw skin.

Then a hand. A head. Two heads. Two more hands.

"Oh, fuck."

***

"The babies have sensors on their feet, usually around one ankle," I murmured, looking as the parents were reunited with their healthy babies. "Caria had access to the tools needed to take them off without setting off the alarm. She's put them on multiple times before."

My heart wasn't in the explanation, though.

No, it was upstairs with my own children who were, as of right now, stable. However, they couldn't have any visitors. The doctor said if all went well through the night that we would be able to visit in the morning during regular visiting hours.

"Can you give me any more information?" Detective Cree asked.

I shook my head.

"You're free to go, then." He gestured to the door with a flick of his hand. "I'm going to question Caria."

I didn't give one flying fuck what she said. The cameras in the stairwell disproved any wrongdoing on Krisney's part, and the damning evidence of Caria walking out of the maternity floor with a bag that just happened to have two newborn babies in it was effectively going to put her away for quite a long fucking time.

Though, she could possibly be paralyzed from the waist down, so there was that, too.

And I couldn't find it in me to care.

"Let's go," I said, holding out my hand for Krisney.

She placed her hand in mine, and together we walked out of the hospital.

***

Two hours, and hundreds of questions later, Krisney and I were sitting on the couch in my living room.

"We need to order some baby stuff," I found myself saying.

Krisney shook her head, and I looked at her. "I don't want to get anything. I want to…wait."

"Krisney…"

"If they…if they don't make it…I don't want the reminder that they didn't."

I didn't have anything to say to that.

I couldn't come up with anything that would make her feel better, because she was right.

Getting baby stuff meant that they were coming home, and there was a slight possibility that they wouldn't make it.

They were so young.

So, so young.

"Okay," I murmured.

"That's stupid," Dante said.

I blinked, surprised to find him standing in my kitchen doorway.

"You're already writing them off," Dante continued as if we'd argued with him. "They're Hails. Fucking fighters. Don't write them off. They're gonna be here. They're gonna come home, and then you'll feel stupid because you should've started to buy shit for them and didn't."

"Can I hold her?" Krisney asked.

Dante didn't hesitate.

Where he did with the rest of us, me included, he handed Mary right over to Krisney as if he'd been doing it from day one.

Dante had always had a soft spot for Krisney.

They'd bonded over ice cream one day and had a special connection ever since.

I didn't understand it and never pretended to.

"She's gotten so big from the last pictures you sent me," Krisney murmured, surprising the shit out of me.

"He's sent you pictures?"

Krisney frowned. "Yeah, he has. Why?"

I looked over to Dante to see that his expression was entirely closed off.

Whatever.

I sighed and rubbed my hands over my eyes.

"You're getting baby shit." He paused. "And I went through your woods with a few friends. Found two more traps. Don't think there are any more, but I'll spend some time out there every once in a while, to make sure."

On that, we were agreed.

I'd already gone out there myself and did a sweep of the area after Pepe had died. I had planned on doing it again myself every spare chance I had, but then Caria carried out her plan to rid me of my pesky family. So, if Dante was offering to head out there again to look around, I'd take him up on it.

I never, not ever, wanted to see that expression on Krisney's face again.

I didn't want to ever see her hurt again.

"Speaking of that old place," Dante continued as if we'd had this discussion hundreds of times.

I immediately shook my head. I didn't want Dante to say anything more. Not yet, anyway.

"Where was Rafe?" I asked.

"Rafe had a little accident last night," Dante said, looking away.

"What kind of accident?" I questioned, tensing.

"The kind where he's incapacitated at the moment."

"What?"

Dante looked away.

"Dante," I growled. "What have you gotten yourself involved in?"

Dante grimaced. "It'll be okay."

Call me crazy, but I didn't fucking believe him.

CHAPTER 23

*I like to have my cake and eat it, too. I also like to have your cake
and eat it, too.*
-Krisney to Reed

Reed

During the days, I spent half of them at work, half of them in the
NICU, and my nights working on my secret project.

It was a bonus that my brothers were helping, too.

The progress we were making meant that we might have a new
house to bring our children to rather than bringing them to my
place, and I was honestly quite excited by the prospect.

It'd been four weeks since the day that our children had a setback,
but ever since, we hadn't had anything else go wrong on their end.
They were thriving.

And today, we were finally, *finally* going to hold our children
without the eight thousand cords and tubes attached to them.

As of eight this morning, they graduated from the endotracheal
tube and the CPAP, which forced air down their windpipes into
their lungs, to just a nasal cannula. The next step would be them
breathing without any assistance.

I couldn't fuckin' wait.

There was practically a skip to my step as I made my way down
one flight of stairs. Each day it came more and more easily until
one day I was no longer getting winded. My body didn't feel any

different than it had before I'd donated my kidney and half of my liver to Krisney, and I was grateful.

That pain was a constant reminder of what had almost happened to her, and it fuckin' hurt to think about. Hurt to breathe. Hurt so bad sometimes that I woke up in the middle of the night with sweat drenching my body.

"Heard you had a big one!"

I looked up to find another labor and delivery nurse headed my way from upstairs.

I grinned. "Sure did. Eleven and a half pounds."

"Yikes!" She giggled as she passed. "Not the biggest, though."

No, it hadn't been. The biggest this hospital had ever seen had been a thirteen-pound baby.

I'd just delivered a baby who was two weeks late and looked like the fuckin' Michelin Man compared to my own, but he was absolutely adorable.

I wondered if our kids would one day have rolls like that. Sure, they were finally starting to get some fat in their cheeks at an adjusted age of thirty-eight weeks, but they were nothin' compared to this baby who had just been delivered—naturally.

Grinning, I stopped at the scrub station and washed up before putting on a gown and a pair booties which were stored there.

Once I was covered from shoulder to mid-calf, I headed inside and grinned at my mom.

"How are they doing?" I asked as I looked around for Krisney.

"She's getting lunch," Mom said, then sighed. "Reed, I'd like to talk to you while she's not here."

I frowned.

My mother and I hadn't had the best of relationships lately.

She felt bad for how she'd acted. I could tell. Yet, I couldn't quite forgive her. I couldn't get over the fact that she tried to guilt me into choosing myself over the woman that everyone knew I loved.

It'd been six weeks, and she was avoiding the issue. She was going on with life like she hadn't said such hurtful things.

"What about?" I asked, moving to the closest baby which happened to be Baxter—who was now in an open-top radiant warmer bed that made handling the babies so much easier while still helping to maintain their body temperatures.

It was a big step.

Dash, though, was still in his incubator, but they expected him to move to a convertible warmer any day now.

"Heya, Bax," I spoke to my son. "Whatcha doin'?"

He turned his head toward me, and I swear I saw a tiny smile grace his features before he craned his neck and squirmed the other way.

Grinning, I moved back to Dash and reached my hand into the opening.

Running my finger down the length of his arm, I smiled at his sleeping form.

"You want to hold them now?"

I nodded, excitement tearing through me, making me bounce in excitement once again.

"It's about feeding time, too," my mother said. "Take a seat, and we'll get Dash for you. When Krisney gets back, we'll get them started on their bottles."

I stripped off my shirt, knowing that they'd allow me to hold him skin-to-skin—what we called kangaroo care—since Dash still wasn't able to maintain his own body temperature completely.

Dash was just under five pounds, and Baxter was an even five pounds.

Both boys were still tiny as hell, but they were getting cuter by the day.

Once I was situated, my mother lowered the sides of the incubator and moved the baby out with practiced ease.

My mother had been doing this for a very, very long time. She'd been in the NICU for as long as I could remember, but there was something about these children being her grandkids that changed her demeanor slightly.

She was confident, sure, but she wasn't as sure of herself as she would normally be.

And I felt that it had a lot to do with me and Krisney rather than them being her grandchildren.

She laid Dash on my chest and then immediately covered me up with a warm blanket, pinning Dash in between my chest and the blanket as she did.

Once she situated his nasal cannula, she reached for Baxter.

The two boys of mine loved being together.

It was like they knew when the other was near, and this time was no different.

Once I flipped the blanket back for my mother to place my other boy on my chest next to Dash, I looked down and grinned.

"Damn, it's nice not to have that big thing weighing your face down," I told the two boys. "I can actually see your cute, little noses."

They felt like tiny weights on my chest, and I wondered if I'd ever get tired of this feeling.

Probably not.

My mother stopped at the side of my chair, and then ran her finger down the length of Baxter's cheek.

"I want to apologize."

I blinked, surprised to see her actually acknowledging that she had a problem.

"I already apologized to Krisney." She swallowed. "It's taken me weeks to realize that what I said and did was stupid." She breathed out deeply then continued. "If I had a chance to talk to your sisters again, I'd tell them that I love them. I'd tell them how I'm always thinking about them and how I wish I could give them each a hug one more time. I'm sorry for the ugly words I said to you before you made such a huge, selfless sacrifice for the woman you love. I'm so sorry, Reed, and I hope that one day you'll forgive me."

I looked down at my two boys, then back up at my mother.

"I know you said some hurtful things," I murmured. "But I didn't take them to heart. I know that you were just hurt and scared." I paused. "But I'm glad you apologized. I didn't realize how much I needed to hear it until you did."

She touched the top of my head, and then dropped a kiss on it. "I have other babies to see to, but if you need help, just holler."

I didn't reply as she walked away, but my heart was somehow healed, even when I didn't know it needed to be.

I guess it showed how mothers knew best.

I sat that way for a good twenty minutes, talking and recounting a story to the boys while I waited for their mother to make it back from lunch.

She didn't take long.

"Seriously, does every cute nurse in the universe have to stop by when you're shirtless?" she asked with a flustered smile on her face.

I looked up to see Krisney hustling toward me, and behind her were three nurses, none of which I knew, staring inside at me.

"What?"

"They're here for you, for your information." She rolled her eyes. "It's like mommy porn."

I shook my head. "I feel like you're high on something."

She snorted and walked up to me, peeking over my shoulder at her two boys.

Baxter opened his eyes at hearing his mother's voice and tried valiantly to lift his head.

It didn't happen, but he was trying and that was all that mattered yet.

"Look at you," Krisney cooed, running her finger down Baxter's cheek. "You're getting so big."

She was right about that. It felt like they changed, even from day-to-day.

They'd been in the NICU now for six weeks and they looked like entirely different babies from the ones that were first brought here.

"Your mom apologize?" Krisney whispered in my ear.

I nodded, not looking at her. "She did."

"Did you accept?"

I nodded.

She pressed her lips to my cheek. "Good."

***

Later that night, I finally had enough of my secret project done that I delegated tasks to my family as well as a few of the men from Hail's Auto Recovery, and I decided to call it an early night.

Krisney didn't know what I was doing in my spare down time, but she didn't ask because I told her it was a surprise.

Ever since she'd gotten out of the hospital, we'd spent quite a lot of time together, so I was sure it was burning her ass not to know what I was doing for two and three hours a night without her.

I expected her to question me on where I'd been, like she always did, when I walked in the door, but found her nowhere to be found.

"Krisney?"

She didn't answer, but I knew she was home. I'd called on my way to ask if she wanted anything to eat. When she'd denied needing the food, I'd assumed she was already cooking, only I didn't find her or dinner in the kitchen waiting for me.

I also didn't find her in the laundry room, the living room or the pantry.

Heading down the hall, I peeked my head into the boys' room which still wasn't furnished but was gathering supplies for the babies for when they did come home, and still didn't see her.

"Kris?" I called again.

Pushing through the open door to my room, I came to a sudden, bone-jarring halt right inside the door, and stared.

"Kris," I croaked.

She was lying on the bed, spread eagle, as she watched me.

"I've decided."

My brows rose. "You've decided?"

She nodded, then trailed a single finger from the tip of her wet tongue, all the way down her throat, down her shoulder, and to one perfectly pink nipple.

As she circled it, she watched me.

"Yes," she confirmed. "I've decided that it's been six weeks, you're healthy. I'm healthy. And I freakin' want you."

My dick was already hard, but at her words, it thickened even further.

There wasn't a single thing in this world that I wanted more.

"I thought you were going to make me wait for our wedding night?" I teased.

She blushed.

"I can't be expected to abstain when you take your freakin' shirt off every time you enter the NICU and hold our boys." She squirmed. "God," she closed her eyes, "there's something wrong with me that all I can think about when I see you hold them is that you're half naked. I should be excited that you can hold them, not thinking about getting you home later that night and doing bad things to you."

"What kind of bad things?" I asked, shuffling closer to the bed.

I hadn't taken anything off yet, but I was about to.

Or at least, I would have had she not spread her legs wider, opening herself up to my gaze.

I growled and kneeled on the bed, my erection straining the front of my scrub bottoms, and leaned forward until my nose was inches from her pussy.

"You know," I said casually as I took a deep breath, smelling her sweet scent. "I can't tell you how many times these past few weeks that I thought about rolling you over until your head hung off the side of the bed."

"W-what?" she asked.

"Yeah," I leaned down and stuck out my tongue, pressing just the very tip of it to her clit.

She jolted.

"What would t-that accomplish?" She squirmed.

"Then I'd get to fuck your throat," I informed her.

She gasped, both at the thought of me fucking her mouth and my thumb pressing against her clit.

"I would've let you," she explained.

I grinned. "I know you would."

Then I ate her, pouring a considerable amount of sexual frustration into reclaiming Krisney's pussy.

I devoured her.

There were no other words for what I did.

One second I was enjoying myself, tasting and licking, and the next she was pulling me up by my overly long hair.

"Can I help you with something?" I rasped, pressing my mouth to hers.

My beard was glistening with her juices, but that didn't bother her in the least as she kissed me back, almost as if she were punishing me for what I'd just done to her, stopping when she was so close.

Yet, I wasn't the one who had stopped—she was by pulling me up by my hair.

Granted, I didn't have to go, but I could tell that she wanted me inside of her.

Hell, I wanted to be there, too.

"Condom." She slapped me on the chest, and a crinkle of the condom wrapper followed the movement.

Grinning, I shucked my shirt over my head by pulling the back of the collar and tossed it down on the bed beside us, before hastily yanking at the fastenings to my scrub bottoms.

It took point four seconds to get it loose and shove them down below my balls, and another ten to get the condom rolled into place.

A few seconds after that, I was sliding home.

"Ahhhh, God." She arched, her pretty pink nipples reaching up into the air. "You feel so good."

She did, too.

But I was finding it hard to breathe, let alone tell her that.

So instead of speaking, I fucked her in hard, deep strokes. Pulling myself almost all the way out before roughly shoving myself back inside.

Over and over until I felt her start to clench around me.

And when she screamed, I watched her fall over the edge into orgasm.

Once she was sated and lying on the mattress below me, I pulled out, ripped off the condom, and stroked my cock until I released all over her stomach. The white come dotted her belly, which was still slightly stretched out from our sons. Stretch marks lined both sides, and I reached forward to rub it all in, paying extra attention to the areas where our sons were more evident.

"What are you doing?"

My eyes flicked up to hers.

"I'm memorizing everything about you all over again." I growled. "Every single day, I find something new about you to love."

CHAPTER 24

Bitches love a man in uniform.
-Reed to Krisney, the day she finds out about his deployment

Reed

The thing about the Reserves is you never know when you'll be called. You never know when your services will be needed.

Lord knows, if my moral code had allowed it, it wouldn't have been three days after my sons were released from the NICU. And it wouldn't have been ten minutes after I was married.

No, it wouldn't have been then, because I was so fuckin' happy I could burst. I wanted to be able to stay here, in my new life, and memorize every single moment.

What I didn't want to do was take over for a doctor that was stationed in fuckin' Germany. The one that I'd been temporarily filling in for when I was there when all of this had started with Krisney and me.

Yet, I couldn't sit well with myself if I didn't help.

I only said, 'Yes, sir.'

My phone had rung ten minutes after saying 'I do.'

Thinking that it was the call center telling me a woman was in labor, I answered it, intending to tell the attendant that Torres was on call for me today.

What I got instead was a man telling me that I was being summoned to take over for a doctor that had been hurt in the line of duty.

"When?" I asked, praying I'd at least get today.

"One week to get your affairs in order," the man on the other end of the line said. "The doc is really hurt. There's no way he's finishing his stint. The next doctor has to close down his practice and was given three months to do so, so you'll be covering for him until he can get over here."

Fuck.

I nodded. "Okay. I'll get ready to go. What time does transport leave?"

"0400 hours on the twenty-second."

Fuck.

"Okay," I said. "I'll be there."

He hung up, and I looked at the closed bedroom door that I'd been standing in front of to take the call.

Fuck.

I shoved the phone back into my pocket and returned to the party, a little less excitement in my step than there had been on my way into the room.

I found my wife in the bedroom with our children.

"Do you like it in here?" I questioned softly from the doorway.

Krisney turned tear-filled eyes toward me. "I love it. I can't believe this was what you'd been doing for these last few months."

She hastily swiped her eyes, and I walked further into the room, wrapping my arms around her.

"I wanted it to be perfect," I whispered. "I wanted it to be everything we'd always wanted."

"It is." She sniffled, burying her face between my pectorals. "It's everything I ever wanted."

I squeezed her a little bit tighter.

It'd officially been ten weeks since the boys were born. Ten weeks since both of us had had our operations to save Krisney's life. Ten weeks of praying, loving and relearning everything there was to know about each other.

I'd had my brothers show her the house an hour before the ceremony started.

And five minutes after the ceremony was supposed to begin, I'd had to go find her, knowing that she was overwhelmed.

I hadn't been wrong.

She'd started crying harder the moment she saw me, and then accused me of trying to make her look splotchy in all of her wedding photos.

I hadn't, but I'd shouldered that blame.

Then I'd picked her up and circled around the outside of the house, dropping her at the end of the stupid black rug that doubled as our faux 'aisle.'

Once my brother, Dante, had her by the arm and settled her, I made my way to the altar and waited for her.

She didn't wait for the music at all. She just hurried toward me, threw her arms around me, and told me she loved me before the opening notes of the wedding march even started.

We were laughing, and she was crying, as Dante just shook his head and made his way to the seat that was saved for him beside my other brother, Baylor, and his wife.

Ten minutes after that, we were husband and wife, and I was kissing the living hell out of her.

Minutes after that, I'd received my phone call and had excused myself.

Which led us to now.

"I can't believe you were able to get all this done." She shook her head. "Reed, this place was crazy bad."

I grinned.

"It was," I agreed. "But I had my brothers helping me, as well as some surprise help from the other men who work for Travis. Did you know that Rafe was once a home inspector for six months?"

She shook her head. "That man is a Jack of all trades."

He was.

She ran her hand over the mobile over Baxter's bed, and grinned as she reached forward and picked something up.

"What's this?"

"A baby monitor called the 'Owlet,'" I said. "When they get off their machines, they'll graduate to that. We can never be too safe with them."

It was a monitor that measured the heartbeat of the baby. If the heartbeat slowed too low, then the alarm would sound on my phone, alerting me to a potential problem. Likely I was being a little too paranoid, but I'd rather be safe than sorry.

"I like it," she murmured, her eyes turning up to meet mine. "I love you, Reed Husband."

I chuckled. "I love you, too, Krisney Wife."

***

It was over six hours later when the last guest finally left, leaving us alone in our newly-refurbished house, on our wedding day.

I was glad for them to be gone, but I was scared to death to tell Krisney after everything that had happened, when we were finally all together, I was given orders to leave.

God, there was nothing in the world that I wanted to do more than be there with my family, but I'd made a commitment, and if there was anyone in this world who would understand that, it was Krisney.

After stripping off my clothes, I took a few moments to collect myself.

Once done, I got up and made my way to the bathroom, brushing my teeth and somewhat trying to contain my hair, before I gave up.

Walking into the kitchen, I looked around and smiled when I saw the mess of bottles, food from last night's rushed dinner, and my scrubs folded neatly on the countertop inches away from a pot containing leftover spaghetti sauce.

Shaking my head, I bypassed the mess and walked into the living room, smiling when I saw my three favorite people on the couch.

Krisney was on the middle couch cushion, her body scrunched forward so the majority of it was lying on the ottoman that was shoved up next to the couch. Both babies were on either side of her in a football hold, feeding each baby from a bottle.

Krisney originally wanted to try to breastfeed, but with the anti-rejection medications she was on for the donor liver and kidney, she hadn't been able to do so.

Now, the boys were completely on donor milk from a multitude of sources, a vast majority of those being from my brothers' wives.

"Babe?"

I looked up from my boys to my wife.

"I need to talk to you." I sighed.

She frowned. "Is it about that phone call you didn't want me to overhear?"

I rolled my eyes.

"Yeah."

"We should probably put some sort of soundproofing in the walls for later on." She grinned, but it quickly fell. "When do you leave?"

"The twenty-second."

She sighed. "Dammit."

I walked around and sat on the ottoman. "My thoughts exactly."

***

One week later

I shouldered my bag and looked down at my little family.

The rest of my family was standing off in the distance, watching me say goodbye to Krisney and our kids without interrupting.

"Baby?"

I grinned down at Kris.

"Yeah, honey?"

"Are you okay?"

I nodded, suddenly nervous.

"I have something to tell you before I go."

Her eyes suddenly took on a shade of nervousness.

"Do you…"

I shook my head and pulled her in closer to me. I knew what she was thinking. She thought that I was saying a 'just in case' kind of thing. In case I died over there like the last doctor almost had.

I wouldn't be doing that. I would be coming home.

"No, baby. That's not what I was going to say."

Relief flooded her tightly-strung body.

"Shit."

I wrapped both arms around her, being mindful of the babies that I was somewhat squishing to get the hug, and pressed my lips to her forehead.

"I love you, Kris," I told her. "I want you to think about something while I'm gone."

Her head tilted up to allow our gazes to meet.

"What is that?"

I pulled back, then dropped my mouth to place on the baby's forehead that was riding on the front left side of Kris's body. Moments later, I moved to the one on the right.

Once I'd gotten a good inhale of their scents, and gave them one more kiss each, I pulled away, and reached for the box in my left front pocket.

"How much I love you."

Her eyes went soft.

"I know that I've been an ass," I said. "I know that I've done things, said things, that weren't always right. But there was always one constant thing in all these years that's separated us. When I get back, I want to have that honeymoon we always talked about. Until then, I want you to read the letters I write. I want you to remember that I love you with my whole heart, and there's not one single thing that I regret about anything since we got back together. I've loved every single second of having you in my life, and I'm glad that I got to experience it with you."

I reached for her hand and brought it to my mouth.

After placing a single chaste kiss on her hand, I turned and walked away.

I got all the way to the door that would lead me to the airplane that would be taking me half a world away from my little family when Kris called out, "I love you, too, Soldier Boy!"

The necklace I'd bought her dangled from her fingers. On it were three words in my messy doctor's script: I love you.

CHAPTER 25

Every corpse on Mount Everest was once an extremely motivated individual. That's why I love my couch. A couch has never killed anybody.
-Krisney to Hennessy

Krisney

Both of the babies were in slings—one on my chest and the other on my back—while we waited for Reed's flight to land.

He'd been gone for three months, and our babies had changed so much.

I was practically giddy to tell him my answer.

He'd left, and I'd been here, burning to tell him yes.

When he'd been informed that he was being deployed to replace a doctor that was hurt it'd been with only one week of notice.

Before I'd had time to come to terms with him leaving, only six and a half days after our wedding, he was boarding the plane that would take him to a layover. Which would then take him to Germany.

Now, two months and eighteen days later, he was on his way back.

I wouldn't lie and say that the last two months and eighteen days had been easy, because they certainly hadn't.

Not only did I have to deal with two babies who were young and in need of so much attention, I had to sell my parents' house.

Luckily, I'd made quite a whack off the money since a new development was coming to Hostel, meaning that they gave me top dollar for my parents' house, only to have them tear it down a week after I sold it to them. With the extra money that I'd made, I'd told the dentist whose practice I'd previously been about to work for to go ahead and move on without me, and I stayed at home with my children and enjoyed their first two months of life without multiple things attached to various parts of their bodies.

Another thing I'd also had to do that was in no way easy for me was to testify in a court of law about what I'd seen that day that Crazy Caria had tried to shoot me in the stairwell of the hospital. The day that she'd also stolen two babies straight out of the nursery in the hospital.

There, I'd learned that Caria had planned on doing much more than just stealing two babies. She'd planned on "taking care" of mine, killing me, and then replacing me and the babies with herself and two random babies she'd stolen.

Caria had pled guilty by reason of insanity and had tried to have herself sentenced to a facility where she'd spend the next eighteen months under the care of a doctor who would 'make her all better.'

Only the judge had surprised everyone by denying her plea for insanity.

The jury had then found her guilty of attempted murder as well as two counts of kidnapping.

She'd sat there, in her wheelchair, looking for all the world like she was dumbfounded.

But her eyes, when they turned to me, had told the entire truth.

She'd thought that she'd get away with what she'd done by pleading insanity, and she'd been completely thunderstruck that she hadn't gotten what she wanted.

After leaving with Travis and Baylor at my side that day, I'd immediately sent an email to Reed on my phone explaining all that had happened.

I hadn't received an email from him since I'd told him, but he'd called only two days ago and said he was coming home. After a quick explanation and flight number exchange, he'd had to go, and I'd been left feeling both nervous and saddened that I hadn't gotten to talk to him longer.

Which led me to now.

I was probably going to hell for this, but I hadn't relayed the information to his family.

So, sue me, I wanted to spend time with him, just us, and didn't think I could accomplish that with his family at my back. All eighteen million of them.

Not that I didn't love all eighteen million of them, but they'd had him for a long time. I'd had him for a short time.

I wanted him to myself.

The first couple of people started to trickle off the plane, likely the first-class passengers, which was where I knew for a fact Reed had been seated when he'd sent me his itinerary.

Frowning, I looked around me to see if I'd missed him and came face to face with Rafe.

"What are you doing here?"

He grinned. "I got off the plane."

"When?"

"Just a second ago."

"Why?"

"Because I was doing something."

"What?"

He grinned. "Noneya."

"Noneya?"

"None ya business."

I snorted.

"Why are you standing right here?"

He looked back toward the terminal. "I want to see your face when you see him."

"Why..."

And then I saw him.

He came off the plane looking pissed off as all get out.

At first, he didn't see me, so I had to leave my perch at Rafe's side and hurry toward him.

Reed's eyes started moving around, and the moment they locked on me, his anger transformed to excitement.

He started hurrying toward me and would've barreled into me had he not stopped at the last second.

"Shit," he said, stopping a few heartbeats short of throwing his arms around me. "This is awkward."

I chuckled and leaned forward, giving him a side hug as I buried my face into his neck.

He smelled like sun, his deodorant, and sweat.

Everything that I loved about him.

"I'm so glad you're home," I whispered.

"Me, too."

"What took you so long to get off the plane?"

"Nothing," he muttered, sounding almost angry again.

"Actually," Rafe said. "He got banished to the back of the plane because some chick kept trying to put her hands down his pants, and he wasn't liking that all that much."

I took a step back, eyes wide, and stared at him.

"What?"

At my angrily exclaimed word, the babies, who'd both been sleeping comfortably in their carriers, woke up with a vengeance.

Honestly, I was surprised they'd been sleeping that long.

They'd been at it all morning—crying, screaming and carrying on.

The doctor said that they were likely about to start teething, and since I had absolutely zero experience with kids, I'd had to take her word for it.

Which led us to the single hour that they'd been asleep in their carriers snuggled close to my body.

I don't know what I expected. They always woke up at the same time.

This time being no different.

Reed being there, however, was.

He was excited as he reached into the carrier wrapped around my back and lifted our son, Dash, out.

Over the two months that Reed had been away, both boys had put on well over six pounds apiece. Now, they were an even eleven pounds for Dash, and twelve pounds one ounce for Baxter.

The minute that Reed brought Dash up to his face and inhaled his sweet baby scent, I fell in love with him all over again.

Dash didn't stop crying, but Reed didn't care. He just hugged him and closed his eyes, memorizing everything about him all over again.

"Y'all have fun with that."

Rafe left after those few short words, and I shook my head. "Did you know he was over there with you?"

Reed nodded. "I saw him a few times, but I never figured out why he was there," he explained, holding his arm out for me.

I took his hand that wasn't cradled around Dash's booty, and started out of the airport hand in hand with my man.

We made it to the car before I got Baxter out, who was still just as pissed now as he was when I'd woken him up.

The moment we were in the truck—Reed's truck—we switched babies.

I smiled when he did the same thing to Baxter as he did to Dash.

"So, tell me about this woman," I ordered.

Reed's eyes went wired.

"I told her if she didn't leave me alone, that I would have my wife kick her ass."

"Oh, really?"

He nodded. "Really."

"Point her out, I'll take care of her sorry ass."

Reed laughed. "Let's get these boys strapped in and head home. I'm dying to be inside of you."

I blushed profusely.

"Reed," I whispered. "You can't say stuff like that in front of those delicate ears."

He snickered. "Didn't you tell me that we needed to fix the insulation between our room and the nursery?"

I nodded.

"Then these words won't be the only thing they hear tonight, unfortunately."

I just shook my head.

"Let's go."

But when we got home, Reed didn't take me to our room.

He stopped dead in the middle of our living room and stared at the mess.

"What..."

Then a dog—who looked exactly like our Pepe—stepped out from behind the recliner.

"So, about that..."

He looked over to me.

"You're in so much trouble."

EPILOGUE

PSA: Due to pregnancy hormones currently surging through my body, I could kiss you or geld you at any moment. Be prepared.
-Text from Krisney to Reed

Reed

Two years later

"Push."

"I don't want to push," she snarled. "If I push, I'll shit all over the fucking table, and then you'll tease me relentlessly for the rest of my life. So no, I'm not pushing. You can go to fuckin' hell."

And that was that.

I rolled my eyes. "Kris, I've seen hundreds of women give birth. I know what the body goes through. I won't judge…"

"You will not do. This. To. Me," she snarled. "*GO* away."

I ignored her and felt the fontanel of my daughter's head—yes, we'd accidentally found this one out at the twenty-week exam— and said with more patience than I'd ever used with any other woman, "Push."

"Fuck. You."

Then she pushed.

And, for all those wondering, no, she did not shit on the table.

She did, however, scream my fuckin' ear off as she dug one of her heels into my shoulder and tried to donkey kick me in the face.

"Oh, my fuckin' God!" she screeched. "Why the fuck did we think it was a good idea to go on a fuckin' babymoon three weeks before my due date?"

That, unfortunately, had been my idea.

But, as her doctor, I'd thought it would be okay.

We were only two hours away. What could go wrong?

Apparently, I didn't factor in the hike that Kris wanted to take, or the goddamn flash flood that rolled over the entire goddamn bottom half of Texas.

No, because if I had, I might not have suggested going to a cabin in the woods with no one around for miles.

I also wouldn't have suggested we go on a weekend where it was set to hurricane the shit out of Texas.

But I had suggested it. And we did go on a hike.

And now, we were stranded when the only two roads leading out of where we were located were washed out. I'd tried to leave earlier, for your information, but Krisney went into hard labor, which led us to now and her currently delivering our third child.

"Fuck you."

I tried not to take her words to heart as she screamed in pain, but just as suddenly as that 'fuck you' had come out of her mouth, she bared down, and our daughter was born kicking and screaming, already acting exactly like her mother.

I caught her with smooth, practiced hands, and fucking smiled like a dolt as I did.

"Oh, God," I breathed. "Baby, she's perfect. Just like our boys."

She had dark brown hair—a lot of it—and squinty eyes. A cute little button nose just like Dash, and a set of lungs like Bax.

Our sons, Dash and Bax, were now two years old. They acted, sounded, and played like other normal two-year-olds. Bax had a slight speech delay, but Dash more than made up for that with talking for both of them. Dash was a late walker, but now you couldn't even tell that he hadn't started to walk until he was well over a year and a half old.

Both boys were happy, healthy, and everything that I ever imagined.

Our new daughter, though, I knew was going to be a force to be reckoned with…just like her mother.

"Can you give her to me already, baby hog?"

Chuckling, I cleaned her off, sucked out her nose with a bulb, and handed her over.

"Aren't you glad I brought my doctor bag now?" I teased.

She rolled her eyes.

Not only had I brought my doctor bag, but I'd packed the car with all the necessities a newborn baby would need…just in case.

And wasn't I now glad I did?

"Yeah, baby." Krisney started to sniffle. "I'm glad you did."

I waited and attended to other matters—such as delivering her placenta and cleaning her up—while she bonded with the baby.

Once everything was as clean as I was going to get it—and no, I doubted we were going to get our deposit back for this one—I rounded the table and picked her up, carrying her to the clean bed.

Once she was settled, I crawled in beside her, pulled out my phone, and called my mother.

She answered on the second ring.

"You got time to Facetime, Mom?"

Facetime had become a thing for me and the boys.

Sometimes I worked late hours and didn't get the chance to say
goodnight to our kids. On those days, I'd Facetime Krisney and
talk to the boys, tell them a bedtime story and give them air kisses.

So, they were not new to this game.

What was new was seeing another person on the receiving end of
their phone call.

"Boys," I turned the phone so it was pointing at Krisney and their
new sister. "I want you to meet your sister, Amy."

Life hadn't gone as planned for Krisney and me.

No, we'd both suffered uselessly, and most of that was my own
doing.

But I was making up for it now with every single breath I took.
The day I died, I wanted Krisney to know that she had meant
everything to me. Hopefully in fifty plus years from now, she
would look back on our time together, and the happiness of our
lives would outweigh the regret over losing those first twelve years
together. Hopefully, when she looked back over our life, she only
thought of the happy years we'd had after we reconnected, and
never felt sad again.

I'd spend the rest of my life making sure that she was happy, and I
would enjoy every single second of it as I did it.

"God, baby," I breathed, looking down at my two girls. "She's
fuckin' perfect."

She glared at me. "Language."

I managed not to point out to her that she'd said enough F words to
last them a lifetime.

"Yes, ma'am."

ABOUT THE AUTHOR

Lani Lynn Vale is the USA TODAY Bestselling Author of over twenty novels. She writes romantic suspense, and loves reading it, too. She is a married mother of three, and lives in Texas on a small farm.

Made in the USA
Monee, IL
15 January 2020